"There's no [...] convince m[...]"

Dominic's deep brown eyes were resolute. Perhaps even sorrowful, but still...stony. Steely. Implacable.

Gianna's heart pounded in her chest. If she didn't convince him to keep the store, where would she go? The only place she could fall back on was her parents' restaurant, and busing tables and packing to-go orders didn't appeal to her.

"I'm giving you an ultimatum!" she said frantically. "Please. Hear me out."

He arched one dark eyebrow at her, looking painfully unimpressed. "Go on."

"The town's annual fair is coming up in two months." She took a deep breath, trying to gather her thoughts. "Why don't you work with me in the store until then? Consider it a trial run. You'll get a feel for the place, how much it brings to the community *and* how profitable it is. If you don't see its value by the end of two months, then you can do whatever you want with it."

He cocked his head to one side. "You've got yourself a deal, Gianna."

Nicole Lam lives in Alberta, Canada, where she spends most of the year indoors, avoiding the frigid winters. She has a BA in English. When she's not writing, you can find her learning different languages, trying new caffeinated drinks and reading about happily-ever-afters.

Books by Nicole Lam

Love Inspired

Saving the Single Dad's Bookstore

Visit the Author Profile page at LoveInspired.com.

Saving the Single Dad's Bookstore

Nicole Lam

LOVE INSPIRED
INSPIRATIONAL ROMANCE

LOVE INSPIRED®
INSPIRATIONAL ROMANCE

ISBN-13: 978-1-335-59857-8

Saving the Single Dad's Bookstore

Love Inspired
22 Adelaide St. West, 41st Floor
Toronto, Ontario M5H 4E3, Canada
www.LoveInspired.com

Printed in U.S.A.

Now our Lord Jesus Christ himself, and God, even our Father, which hath loved us, and hath given us everlasting consolation and good hope through grace, Comfort your hearts, and stablish you in every good word and work.
—*2 Thessalonians* 2:16–17

To Fiza.

Chapter One

When Gianna Marchesi walked into Tang's Terrific Tomes at eleven thirty on a Saturday morning, she didn't expect to find it full of men in hard hats and yellow vests. Nor did she anticipate seeing the tall Asian man leaning against the counter with confident ease. He was giving orders to the workers and seemed to be eyeing the bookshop for a renovation, or worse, a complete teardown.

The store opened at noon on the weekends, and only she and the owner had the keys. But today, unfamiliar men with tape measures swarmed Tang's familiar curved bookshelves, which she had lovingly arranged into neat alcoves with comfy chairs. Workers in steel-toed boots trampled the colorful rugs in the nook where children sat for reading hours.

Worst of all, someone was standing in the place *she* always occupied, leaving Gianna in a state of confusion.

Tang's owner, Philip, had passed recently, but she had fond memories of the older gentleman. He had always brought her tea and often invited her to dinner with him and his wife. However, despite plenty of speculation from Crabtree's citizens, no one knew who the shop had passed to. Was *this* the new owner?

The thought made her heart do an unsettling flip.

"Excuse me." Still standing in the doorway, Gianna cleared her throat when the man didn't hear her. "Excuse me!"

She marched toward the counter in her sensible block heels, which brought her height up from a diminutive five foot three to a respectable five foot six. After she reached the checkout counter, Gianna rang the bell reserved for customers. It got his attention, and he turned to look at her, pivoting away from asking a worker about the height of the ceiling.

"How can I help you?" He was handsome: unruly black hair, sharp jawline with a hint of scruff, well over six feet and with dark eyes that seemed to observe far too much. Or maybe it was because she'd come into the shop on a Saturday expecting far less clamor and commotion. His presence seemed to fill the entire space of the cozy bookshop.

"I'm the manager here. I came to open the shop, but I see you've already done that, Mr....?" If this was one of Philip's lawyers, Gianna would have to tread carefully.

"Dominic Tang." He extended his hand, giving her a polite smile. "I'm Philip's grandson."

"Gianna Marchesi." She smiled back, her expression tight as she shook his hand. Come to think of it, he looked familiar. Remembering her manners, she gave him her genuine condolences. "I'm sorry for your loss."

Philip Tang's recent death had been a shock to everyone in the town. He had been a regular at Gianna's parents' Italian-Chinese fusion restaurant and had been known to sit in the town square feeding the birds. He'd always had a kind word for everybody. The man had been a clear embodiment of God's love to all of Crabtree.

"Thank you." Dominic cast an appraising eye around the bookstore. "You've managed the shop well."

Gianna straightened. "Yes, I've been in charge of redecorating the place and ordering new inventory. We host many town events here—reading hours for children, literacy programs and even arts and crafts. Would you like me to give you a tour?"

"There won't be any need for that. I'm going to be gutting the store and leasing out the space in a matter of weeks," he said.

She felt the blood drain from her face. "*G-gutting* the store?"

Had she heard him right? Was Philip Tang's grandson going to be tearing down Crabtree's most beloved bookstore?

"Yes," he said; his tone sounded like he was answering a question about the time of day or whether the sun was shining. "Do you have any objections to that, Miss Marchesi?"

"Yes!" Before she could say something rash, Gianna took a deep breath. "This store is a fixture of this town! Everyone in Crabtree Point loves the place. *I* love this shop, and I've never worked anywhere else. You can't just waltz into town for five seconds and then destroy one of its landmarks! Tang's is… It's *everything.*"

Her voice caught on the last syllable, and she realized she had said far too much. Tang's was not merely a place of business to her, but almost a second home. It was where she'd worked for years. While her other classmates had moved on to big-city jobs in Edmonton or Calgary, Gianna had poured her heart and soul into this store.

Apparently, she ought to have prayed for the right words to say because sentimentality didn't seem to convince Dominic Tang. He looked like a calculating man of business, even as he wore that cordial smile.

"Miss Marchesi, if your concern is for your future, I assure you, you'll get a glowing reference and a generous severance package from me." Dominic rolled his shoulders back. "Now, if you'll excuse me, I have to go back to work."

Was he dismissing her so soon?

"I came *here* to work." She coughed, not wanting to show him the tears that were close to welling up in her dark eyes. "I'm the manager."

"I own the store now," he said. "I inherited it in my grandfather's will."

"But I've been working here for five years," Gianna murmured. Even if he didn't care about the town, didn't he care about his grandfather's employees? "I took this job straight out of high school. There's nowhere else for me to go."

His gaze seemed to soften at her words, but it may only have been wishful thinking. "Miss Marchesi—"

Hoping to convince him, she blurted out, "Call me Gianna."

"Gianna, my decision has been made. I'm sorry, but there's nothing you can say to convince me." His deep brown eyes were resolute. Perhaps even sorrowful, but still…stony. Steely. Implacable.

Her heart pounded in her chest, and perspiration formed on her palms. If she didn't convince him to keep the store, where would she go? The only place she'd worked besides the bookstore was her parents' restaurant, which was a fusion of her mom's Chinese and her dad's Italian backgrounds. Crabtree being a small town, job opportunities were few compared to bigger cities in the province, and she didn't relish the idea of moving away from her family and friends. The only place she could go was Marchesi's, and hot, sticky summer nights spent bussing tables and packing to-go orders didn't appeal to her.

"I'll give you an ultimatum!" she said frantically. "Please. Hear me out."

He arched one dark eyebrow at her, looking painfully unimpressed. "Go on."

"The town's annual fair is coming up in two months." She took a deep breath, trying to gather her thoughts into some semblance of a functional plan. "Why don't you work with me in the store until then? Consider it a trial run. You'll get a feel for the place, see how it's run, how much it brings to the community *and* how profitable it is. If you don't see its value by the end of two months, then you can do whatever you want with it."

He cocked his head to one side. "You've got yourself a deal, Gianna."

After sending the workers out of the bookstore and deciding to close it early, he'd given himself the rest of the day to think about his next career steps. For now, though, he let himself take a deep breath. Dominic inhaled the fresh mountain air as he walked up his parents' driveway. Nestled in the foothills of the Canadian Rockies, Crabtree was about an hour's drive from other mountain towns like Banff and Jasper. The houses resembled log cabins more often than not, and the streets were named after wildlife like caribou or grizzly bears. Local townsfolk prided themselves on the close-knit community, the abundance of churches and the plethora of restaurants.

Though it should've been a relaxing reprieve from the bustle of Toronto, the city where he'd spent the last seven years, the quiet atmosphere of Crabtree was a reminder of the financial reasons he was here. He'd only spent a few days back in his hometown, but they had been far more emotional than expected. Dominic hadn't realized how much being in Crabtree would remind him of the past—particularly the woman who had left him and their son. After seven years, those memories no longer pained him; they were a glimmer of loss for the family he and Emmett might have had.

His heated disagreement with Gianna Marchesi hadn't helped him relax. On top of that, he'd just lost his job last week due to new management at the accounting firm where he'd been working for the last five years. Therefore, this trip was less of an impromptu vacation and more of a desperate effort to get back on his feet.

"Daddy!" Emmett ran at him, leaping into his arms the second Dominic stepped onto the porch of his parents' home.

He bent down and embraced the seven-year-old boy.

"Hi, Emmett," he said, ruffling his son's hair. "How are you? I hope you didn't tire out your grandparents too much."

"Nope! Me and Grandpa were playing Chinese checkers, and he taught me tai chi. Then Grandma made me help her in the kitchen, and we made scallion pancakes, but I ate them all."

Dominic didn't bother correcting his son's grammar, knowing his mother—a former substitute English teacher—would have done so already. "Sounds like you had a lot of fun, buddy."

The mouthwatering aroma of oil sizzling in a wok wafted toward him as they went through the all-too-familiar front door, a wreath of pink flowers circling the peephole. It mingled with the lemongrass candles that his mother burned, which would always remind him of Crabtree. Well, that, and Marchesi's, the *only* place in town where one could have a proper meal, according to his parents.

"Did you get everything done at the bookstore?" his father asked. "You were out for longer than I expected. Your mother was worried."

"The manager put up a bit of a fight." He ran a hand through his hair, the other hand on Emmett's shoulder. His mother still decorated the foyer with porcelain figurines and delicate vases, and he wouldn't put it past his son to show off his karate and parkour skills to his grandparents. "I guess she objected to my emptying out her place of employment, which is understandable, if inconvenient. I'll have to stick around until the annual fair to work through that."

Gianna Marchesi had thrown a wrench in his plans to gut the store, turn it into office space and then head back to Toronto to find another job. *Inconvenient* was putting it mildly. Yet there was something about her that he couldn't help but be intrigued by. Why did she care so much about the old bookstore?

"Dominic!" His mother came out of the kitchen when she heard his voice. It wasn't as if he hadn't seen her last night when he'd driven up from Calgary, but she was acting like it had been years since they'd reunited. It *had* been almost a decade since he'd set foot in Crabtree, but his parents had flown east to see him in the intervening years. "Oh, I can't tell you how happy I am that you're home."

He let go of Emmett and wrapped his arms

around his mother, or rather, responded instinctively to the tight embrace she was giving him. Dominic chose his next words with caution, not wanting to lie. It *was* good to be back with his parents, but he couldn't say the same for the rest of the townspeople. "Emmett and I are happy to see you and Dad, too."

"Now, what's this you said about employment?" asked his mother, a petite woman with more wisdom and tenacity in her littlest finger than most people had in their whole body. "I hope you were only joking about tearing down the bookstore, Dom. Your grandfather loved that place. It's the heart of the town, right after the church and Marchesi's."

He wanted to avoid disappointing his mother with further discussion about his plans to gut the bookstore, so he changed the subject.

"I'm staying in Crabtree…for now. Speaking of Marchesi's, I'm starving." Dominic crouched down, turning to Emmett, who was practicing a dangerously high kick that nearly toppled the nearby entry table. He grabbed his son's arm and kept him from destroying the furniture. "Are you hungry, bud?"

Emmett nodded frantically, despite having just confessed to eating. He possessed the ravenous appetite of all seven-year-old boys. "I could eat a whole entire *elephant*."

Dominic chuckled at his son's exaggeration. "Why don't we all talk about Tang's over a good meal at Marchesi's? It'll be my treat."

"That sounds great, son," his father said. "You can tell us how it feels to be back."

During the past seven years, he'd been lonely. Hurt. Lost. But God had redeemed him and would carry him through this. He just had to make it to the end of summer, and he could go back to his life: him and his son, with the gossiping, meddling townsfolk of Crabtree nowhere in sight.

Chapter Two

If there was one eternal truth, it was that the food at Marchesi's could cheer up even the most forlorn of broken hearts. Their baked seafood pasta was Gianna's favorite, and the Italian-Chinese mix of rice noodles and spaghetti was unconventional, yet delicious.

The summer after graduating from high school, she had helped out at the restaurant after her father had broken his leg falling off a ladder while taking down the Christmas decorations they'd left up until March. That had delayed her ideas of going to Calgary or Edmonton for art school or at least to pursue something greater than waitressing or working at the bookstore. She'd never had any great interest in college, preferring to do most of her learning through books, but even if she had, she liked it in Crabtree. The sense of community, the multitude of restaurants and boutiques that couldn't be found anywhere else, and the friends and family she'd known all her life compelled her to stay. Not that people didn't leave Crabtree—quite a few did, for work or to marry a tourist they'd met who'd driven through—but she couldn't imagine living anywhere else.

So it was with a slightly peppier step that Gianna slid behind the counter of Marchesi's, where her mother was packing to-go orders and her father was in the kitchen. Her younger sister, Estella, was bussing tables, and Luca, her older brother, was working the floor. Each of her family members greeted her with a wave, a smile or, in her mother's case, a kiss on the cheek. Surprise and curiosity filled their eyes, and she knew the news of Dominic Tang's arrival in town wouldn't remain secret for long. In Crabtree, nothing did.

"Hello, Mama." She closed a take-out box and bagged it, sticking on the receipt with practiced motions. Gianna had grown up in Marchesi's. Her earliest memories were in this restaurant, but that didn't mean she wanted her last ones to be here, too. "How are you?"

"If you're going to be working here like

your siblings, put your hair up at least." Her mother put her hands on her hips as she looked at Gianna. "Did something happen at Tang's? Why aren't you at work?"

"There's a new owner. Philip's grandson Dominic," she said, explaining the story of her unpleasant encounter with the bookstore's new proprietor as she twisted her hair into a messy bun. Gianna had spent the last five years of her life pouring every drop of herself into the store, and Philip Tang had been like a second grandfather to her. Tang's was more than a store—it had been a refuge for her growing up amidst the hectic frenzy of a large family who ran the most popular restaurant in town. "Mama, he wants to gut the entire store! Where will I work? What about the children's reading hour? How can he just *gut* Tang's? What am I going to do?"

She tried to picture a life without Tang's. It felt empty, devoid of her most cherished moments. The drudgery of chopping vegetables and wiping down tables at the restaurant made her shudder even in the spring heat.

Her mother was silent for a moment, packing take-out boxes with smooth motions. "You know, it wouldn't be the worst thing for you to come back and work with us, dear."

Gianna's stomach sank, heavy with guilt. Of course, she should be grateful to be able to work at the restaurant. But the bookstore had been her passion, and it wasn't something she could just walk away from. Even if it had Philip—and Dominic—Tang's name on it. It wasn't simply about having a job and an identity outside her family. Working at Tang's had made her feel like she mattered, instead of being just another Marchesi in town. "That's all you have to say?"

"Dominic…" her mother murmured. "Dominic Tang… Now, where have I heard that name before?"

Nancy Marchesi—née Ko—prided herself on knowing everyone who lived, died or was born in Crabtree. It wasn't difficult when all of them made their way through Marchesi's at some point.

"Luca!" her mother said as he came toward them in search of a take-out box. "Luca, didn't you used to play basketball with a Dominic?"

"That was almost ten years ago, Mama." Luca snagged a container and a paper bag, eager to get back to work. He shrugged off the question about his old classmate.

"You didn't answer my question."

Her older brother brushed an impatient hand through his hair as he shifted his feet. "Dominic got into some trouble in his last year of college. Of course I remember him."

A frown furrowed Gianna's brows. Being three years younger than Luca, she didn't know the same people he did. By the time she had started high school, Dominic Tang and Luca would have graduated.

"Ah." Her mother nodded. "I see. Well, get back to work, Luca."

Her brother scurried off to bring the take-out box to one of his tables. Her mother shoved a stack of menus at her, gesturing Gianna toward the hostess stand.

The door opened, and Gianna nearly dropped the menus in her hands.

Because in walked Dominic Tang, holding a little boy's hand.

Dominic Tang had thought he was immune to gossip.

Considering he had left Crabtree Point with an infant son in tow, after his fiancée had abruptly left him, he had never expected to come back. He *had* expected to be spoken about. It had left a deep gouge mark in him when he'd torn himself away from Crabtree, and he'd spent the few years trying to let the wound close over.

Dominic didn't need anyone—neither their validation nor their opinions—and he wouldn't let them hurt Emmett.

At least, that was what he told himself.

"Dad, why are those people looking at us?" Emmett glanced up at him, dropping his father's hand to scratch the back of his neck.

"They're not," he said, thinking that maybe, just maybe, he wasn't so immune to gossip after all. All he needed was to get through this visit and get back to Toronto as soon as possible. Even if he *had* just made a deal with Gianna Marchesi that would complicate his original plans.

He wanted to shield his son from the gossip, but it was next to impossible. He'd have to settle for distracting him from it.

"Yes, they are—" his son began to say, but stopped when he spotted his grandparents seated in a booth.

Dominic had spent ten minutes hunting for a parking spot after dropping off his parents in front of Marchesi's, and if he was being honest, he'd spent more time than necessary trying to talk himself into stepping foot in the restaurant. Even prayer hadn't assuaged the burning anxiety in his chest as he slid into the booth across from his father and next to Emmett.

The popular restaurant was still just as full as it had been when he'd left all those years ago. He may have acquired a few gray hairs between the ages of twenty and twenty-seven, but Marchesi's was the same. Not shabbier or well-worn, but well loved, familiar, settled. It contained the same worn leather booths, romantic wrought iron chairs with red leather seats and a menu that was written in Chinese, Italian and English.

"Hi, what can I get you to drink?" asked the brunette waitress standing at his table with a notepad and pen in her hand. He was certain he had met her only hours ago, and her name tag confirmed his suspicions. "Water, tea, juice, coffee?"

"Aren't you the bookstore manager?" His brows rose when Gianna Marchesi had the decency to blush, her cheeks turning a pale pink that stood out behind her smattering of freckles. Her sheepish expression was framed by the chestnut strands slipping out of her braid. "I hadn't realized job turnover was so fast in Crabtree that you could work at the bookstore in the morning and be at Marchesi's for lunch."

"Dom!" His mother's scolding tone reached his ears. "I thought I raised you to have better manners than that."

"It's okay, Mrs. Tang. This is my family's business. I'm just helping them since you seem to have the bookstore well in hand, Mr. Tang." Gianna gave him a smile that he was 90 percent sure was fake. Yet he couldn't help but notice the way it made her brown eyes glow.

"What bookstore, Dad?" Emmett said, turning to him with wide eyes that brightened at the mention of books. His son was a voracious reader and would devour anything with text printed on it: comic books, magazines and, occasionally, even the backs of shampoo bottles.

"I'll tell you about it later, okay, buddy?" Then, turning back to Gianna, he said, "We'll have two glasses of water, a black coffee and an orange juice, please."

"Hmm," she said, scribbling down his order before tucking the notepad into the apron tied around her slender waist. She was petite, probably a good head shorter than him, but he got the sense she wasn't a woman he should mess with. "I'll be right back with that."

"Wait," he said before he could stop himself. "What was that *hmm* for?"

"Nothing." Then she seemed to reconsider

her answer. "You just seem like the type to order a plain black coffee. And even more than that, you seem like just the type of guy who would make decisions without asking anyone else for their opinion."

With that, she turned around and walked toward the kitchen, leaving him wide-eyed and more than a little curious.

Who was Gianna Marchesi, and why did he care?

Chapter Three

Gianna's hands shook as she walked back into the kitchen.

Did she just say those words to Dominic Tang, the man who now owned her bookstore? Well, it wasn't *her* bookstore, and never had been, but it had always felt like hers. Philip Tang had had a way of making everyone who walked in feel at home. Horror welled up inside of her at the thought of the store becoming just another soulless concrete block.

She brought out their drink orders, setting them down with a smile that felt like it might drop from her face faster than the Tang's Terrific Tomes sign would come down. "Here you go."

"Thank you." Dominic took the two waters and slid them toward his parents.

"Dad, what bookstore were you talking about?" The young boy seated next to Dominic tugged at his father's sleeve, his face lit up with excitement. "I want to see it!"

"Emmett." Dominic passed him his orange juice, his tone containing more than a warning.

Emmett pouted, though his hand dropped from his father's sleeve. "Dad, please? Can I go see it?"

"I'd love to give you a tour after lunch," Gianna blurted out. "I love the bookstore, too. It's a shame your father doesn't seem to feel the same way."

"Really?" Emmett's eyes widened. "You would do that, Ms. Marchesi?"

"You can call me Gianna. And, of course," she said. "I love showing Crabtree's newcomers around the store."

"Gianna!" Luca called. "Can you come here for a moment, please?"

She hurried over with a tray in hand. "What is it?"

"Take this to-go order over to Mrs. Giovanni. She's been waiting for ten minutes now. And we're too swamped to be making conversation with the customers." Luca shoved two heavy paper bags laden with food into her hands.

Taking the hint, she spent the rest of the hour with one eye on the table of Tangs and another on the clock. Finally, her lunch shift at Marchesi's was over when the Tangs finished eating. She kissed her mother good-bye, waved to her siblings and picked up her keys to make her way toward Tang's.

Gianna arrived at the bookstore a few minutes before Dominic and his son, and she spent the time trying to make the shop as presentable as possible, dusting off the shelves and rearranging the furniture that had been shifted by the workers that were present that morning. At last, when the store more closely resembled the quaint oasis it had been since she was a child, the bell jingled, and Dominic and Emmett walked in.

"Welcome to Tang's Terrific Tomes," she said, hurrying over to the door.

Emmett gazed around the bookstore as though he had walked into a candy shop or a video-game store. She wasn't too sure what boys his age normally liked, but she didn't think she'd ever seen such an expression on any of the Crabtree children's faces upon entering the store.

"You like books, huh?" she said with a

smile. Gianna always loved to see kids show a love for reading at such a young age.

"He loves reading," Dominic answered for his son, as Emmett let go of his hand and ran toward a section of shelves displaying comic books interspersed with action-hero figurines. Gianna had set up that display herself, though she didn't read many superhero comics. The kids who came into the store always made a beeline for it, and from there, many of them moved on to other books.

"This place is awesome, Dad! Wait, do you own it? Is that why it's called Tang's?" he said, running his small hands over the spines on another bookshelf.

For the first time since they had met, Dominic Tang looked speechless, rubbing the back of his neck. His expression was sheepish, like that of a child caught in a lie. The image of him as a little boy who'd broken an expensive vase made her want to smile. If only he wasn't the man promising to tear down the place.

"It's complicated," he said, before turning to her. "Listen, Gianna, can I talk to you for a second?"

She nodded, waving him toward the office in the back of the store. "Of course."

Gianna hoped he had changed his mind,

or at the very least, that his son's enthusiasm had softened it.

"I want to look at the accounts," he said. "I'm not in the best financial shape right now, and I don't want to get into more money trouble."

Her gut clenched. "Of course. I'll have those sent over to you right away."

Just when she hoped he would move on, he spoke again with a frown. "Why do you care about the bookstore so much? You clearly have a backup plan—your family restaurant."

"I'm not working at Marchesi's." She tipped her chin up, her jaw tightening as she stared him down. Or tried to.

Dominic was more implacable than she'd thought. "I could've sworn you just served me lunch there."

This man is infuriating. "What I mean is, I'd prefer to keep my position at Tang's instead of being just another cog in the well-greased Marchesi's machine."

"Fair enough." He tilted his head to one side as he pondered her words.

"Now, *I* have a question for you. Why do you want the bookstore to be some clinical office space? What's wrong with keeping the business as is?"

"I don't want to move back to Crabtree." His voice turned icy.

"What's wrong with it?" He'd grown up here, too, hadn't he?

Dominic scoffed. "Are you kidding, Gianna? This town —"

What was so wrong with her hometown?

"Well, moving on," she said, plastering on a smile reserved for difficult customers who demanded refunds on books they'd annotated and dog-eared. "Is that the only reason?"

He sighed, looking torn about whether to tell her. The talkative side of him—if such a side existed—must have won out. "I was laid off from my job in Toronto a few weeks ago. A bookstore isn't the most profitable business these days, so you'll understand my motives. Two months is more than I want to give this place."

It's more than I want to give you, his words seemed to imply.

She steeled herself. "Thank you for your honesty."

As they exited the office, he added, "Please don't forget to send me those accounts. I want to make sure I haven't inherited a bookstore that's on the verge of financial ruin."

His last words sent a chill down her spine.

* * *

"Dad, I can't believe you own a bookstore and you didn't tell me!" On the way home, Emmett looked at him with a betrayed expression that made Dominic feel like he'd done something wrong.

Gritting his teeth, he drove past the old bowling alley where he had taken Emmett's mother, Carly, on a date. Once, it had felt like some kind of landmark, a memorial to the wreck of their relationship. Now, after all these years, he couldn't bring himself to feel a thing about any reminders of her. All he wanted was to be the best father he could be to Emmett, and that didn't include dwelling on the past. Not when he had so many problems—including Gianna Marchesi, a thorn in his side who somehow made him open up more than he had to his son—to worry about in the present.

Growing up, his own father had never had much time for him. As a child, Dominic had resented the engineering job that had taken his father away for extended stretches of time, forcing him to go to Fort McMurray or other places farther up north in Alberta to work. When he was older, though, he looked back and found himself grateful for the ways his father had provided for their family and the sacrifices he had made in order to give him and his mother a stable life. Yet it had often made him wonder whether he was capable of doing the same for his son. He wondered whether the decision to take on this bookstore would be the wrong choice.

His son's question revived the same doubts in his mind. "I didn't know I was inheriting it until your great-grandpa died."

"But he died two months ago. Didn't you know about the bookstore then?" Emmett pressed.

"Emmett, the lawyers didn't read the will until a few weeks ago. A bookstore is an enormous responsibility, and I couldn't just uproot our whole lives because of it." He flipped the blinker to turn left. "Besides, I haven't decided if I'm keeping it yet."

"But why?"

He sighed. "The bookstore is here. In Crabtree. We have a life in Toronto to get back to."

Even after all this time, being in Crabtree was like a reminder of all his mistakes. Not that he would ever call his son a mistake, but he knew better now than to repeat the past. Even though God had forgiven him for his past sins, coming home didn't feel like redemption; it felt like a pair of too-tight shoes that no longer fit, pinching at the toes.

Or maybe he was reading judgment into the eyes of everyone he passed, still believing that his actions could not be forgiven. No. That wasn't true. Emmett was not a sin. His son—the precocious, kind, energetic, lovable boy in the back seat—could never be anything but a blessing.

"Dad?" Emmett said, sounding like he had been repeating himself for a while now. "Dad, the light changed already."

He shook his head and turned left. "Sorry, kiddo. Guess I just have a lot on my mind today."

"Why don't you want to keep the bookstore?"

"I already told you why." Emmett was too stubborn for his own good sometimes.

"I heard you and Gianna talking about it."

Gianna Marchesi. No woman had intrigued him so much in the last seven years, not even Carly. With his ex-fiancée, their relationship had been simple, easy; they'd been two kids in college, mistaking infatuation for love. Her abandonment of him and their son no longer stung, and he'd long since forgiven her.

Gianna wasn't as simple; she didn't seem

to care about the bookstore just because she wanted to keep her job. If she lost the bookstore, she could fall back on working at her parents' restaurant, no matter how much she didn't want to. So what was it that made her love Tang's so much?

"I'm considering what to do with the bookstore," he said as he pulled into his parents' driveway. "But that's not something you need to worry about, okay?"

"How long are we going to stay in Crabtree, Dad?"

"Missing your friends?" he asked as he shut off the ignition.

In the rearview mirror, his son slumped against the car seat and shook his head. "I like being here with Grandma and Grandpa. I don't want to go back to Toronto. There's never anything to do there."

"Well, I told you we'll be staying here for two months at least, depending on how things go with the bookstore."

Despite all my attempts to leave it.

After she left the bungalow she shared with three housemates, Gianna made her way to her parents' house for their weekly family dinner. On the drive over, Gianna wondered why she felt as if her entire world was collapsing around her. She mulled it over all evening, so engrossed by her fear of losing the bookstore that she barely looked up from her plate of fettuccine. It was her father's turn to cook that night, and he always made Italian food. Gianna busied herself with eating and tuned out her family's voices. That was, until she heard Dominic's name.

"Luca, you know it's not good to gossip," her mother scolded her brother as she twirled a strand of pasta around her chopsticks.

Luca looked sheepish. "Mom, I was just telling Estella and Gianna about Dominic Tang. They didn't go to high school at the same time as me and Dom, so I thought I would enlighten them on the subject. I mean, you're curious, aren't you, G?"

Gianna put down her chopsticks. "Um… sure."

"See?" Luca pointed at her like she would absolve him from the sin of gossiping.

As the middle child in a large, rowdy, Chinese-Italian family comprised of seventeen cousins, eight aunts and uncles, and far too many gossiping busybodies, Gianna knew when to keep quiet. It was also easy when you were often ignored. In addition, she and

Estella were only two years apart, and growing up, people often mistook them for twins. It made Gianna feel like yet another faceless member of the Marchesi clan.

In high school, she'd been bullied as the less popular of the Marchesi sisters, unlike Estella. Her volleyball-playing, lip-gloss-wearing, party-going younger sister had skipped a grade in elementary school, made friends with everyone she met and made Gianna look like a dowdy bookworm in comparison. After graduation, the constant comparisons between them had relented somewhat, but she couldn't help but always feel second-best to her younger sister, a pale moon to Estella's glowing sun. She'd quit working at Marchesi's not only to get out of the kitchen, but also to get out of Estella's shadow. If the bookstore failed, she'd be back to being a nobody—not even significant in her own family, let alone the whole town.

"Gianna wasn't even paying attention," Estella said. "Come on, she doesn't care about your old basketball buddy, Luca."

Gianna was also used to being talked over in a house of larger-than-life personalities. "I care—"

"That's right, Dominic Tang is taking over

the bookstore now, isn't he?" her father, Alberto Marchesi, said. "What's he like?"

She didn't even bother asking how he knew about Dominic's arrival and ownership of the bookstore. No doubt her mother had told him.

Since her father's question wasn't addressed to anyone in particular, she expected one of her siblings to pipe up with a snarky remark. Instead, the room fell silent.

"He's... He's a good dad," Gianna said.

This much seemed to be true. No matter how she felt about his business decisions, there was no denying that he cared for Emmett.

"That's it?" Estella said, her dismissive tone changing to one of curiosity. "He's a good dad?"

"He wanted to gut the bookstore and turn it into an office space. But when he saw how much his son loved the place, well, he seemed to change his mind."

Her mother's eyes narrowed. "Well, I see why he would want to leave Crabtree. This town must hold many painful memories for him."

Seated on her left, Luca muttered, "Didn't she just tell me not to gossip?"

Gianna bit back a laugh, spooning broccoli onto her plate.

"His girlfriend—no, fiancée—left him just a few months after their son was born. She hasn't been seen in Crabtree since," their mother continued.

"You make it sound like she's a ghost." Estella chuckled.

"Well, Dominic has agreed to work with me in the bookstore until the fair, to see if he wants to keep it."

Every year, Crabtree held a fair for small businesses, home bakers and cooks, and anyone who had a gift to share with the community. The small businesses had their own special prizes, one of them being fifteen thousand dollars to the enterprise that had done the most for Crabtree's community that year. The panel of judges was filled with people from different industries in the small town, and no one knew who the judges were until the day of the fair.

Their father sighed. "Whatever happens to the bookstore, Gianna, just know you always have a place at Marchesi's."

"I'm not going back to the restaurant. I don't care *what* happens," she said.

"Bookstores aren't the most profitable businesses these days, especially with big chain bookstores around. Your father is just trying to look out for your future," her mother said soothingly. But it felt more patronizing than comforting, reminding Gianna of what Dominic had already told her today.

Her father glowered at her. "If Dominic Tang decides not to keep the bookstore after the fair, you'll be working at Marchesi's."

"Fine. But he *will* decide to keep it." The reckless words streamed from her lips, and she immediately regretted them.

She sank into her chair, but her heart rose in her chest with renewed vigor. Though she knew her father wanted to be reassuring, it only rooted her deeper in her determination to save Tang's from the hands of calculating businessmen. No matter what she had to do, she would *not* give up on the bookstore.

Chapter Four

Looking up as he finished his prayer, Dominic scanned the pews for any sign of his son. Dominic and his family had been going to the same church all his life, minus the last decade, and even when he'd been subjected to gossip when he'd returned from college with a pregnant fiancée in tow, he'd never skipped any Sundays. However, now church meant more to him. It was no longer just another day in the calendar, but a genuine time of communion and worship with fellow believers.

If only his fellow parishioners felt the same way. Dominic could sense their gazes on him as he scanned the pews again for any sign that the children's worship was over, but he couldn't find Emmett running around anywhere.

As though reading his mind, his mother tapped him on the shoulder. "The children's worship doesn't end for another half an hour. Why not talk to people? You haven't been very social since arriving back in town."

He sighed. "Maybe it would be easier to be social if people were more polite."

"What do you mean? Everyone's been plenty polite. Well, besides Thea Mulcair. I'll admit that her question was out of line—"

"Mom, it's not just Thea Mulcair. It's everyone. If they could discuss something other than the circumstances of my son's birth, which happened seven years ago, I'd be social. If not, well…" He shrugged.

"Naturally, people are going to be curious, honey. You've been gone for ages. Isn't that right, Marcus?" She nudged her husband.

"Yes, whatever you say, Livvy," his father mumbled, too engrossed in rooting through his pockets for something. "Have you seen my—oh, there it is."

He emerged victorious with a wrapped caramel, then offered it to Dominic. "For Emmett."

Dominic tucked the hard candy into his pocket. "Thanks, Dad."

"And, Dom, your mother is right. It wouldn't

hurt to get out there and mingle a bit with the young people instead of staying in the back row with the old fuddy-duddies like me and your mom." Marcus Tang clapped him on the back. "You're young! Get out there."

Egged on by his parents' urging, Dominic groaned and made his way toward the church lobby, hoping to spot a friendly face. People were gathered around the refreshments table, chatting and laughing.

His gaze locked with Luca's, and the other man's eyes widened in surprise as he crossed the room. "Dom! I didn't expect to see you here today."

"You know me. Rain or shine, I'll be here on a Sunday," he said with a forced chuckle. Maybe it would be easier to talk to Luca than anyone else. They were friends once, though their friendship had dissolved in the drama of his failed romance and subsequent child with Carly.

He and Luca had fallen out of touch since Dominic's abrupt departure with Emmett after university graduation. Dominic had wanted to leave behind the heartbreak he'd felt when Carly had told him she couldn't do *this*, gesturing toward Emmett crying in his crib as a symbol of all that she couldn't handle. He'd watched her walk out of the sparsely decorated nursery in the small bungalow they'd rented a few months before she'd given birth. A few weeks later, she'd left permanently, leaving a note telling him that she was overwhelmed by having a child and had never wanted the responsibility of such a monumental role.

The engagement ring she'd left at the front door only confirmed that.

"So, my sister told me you own the bookstore now," said Luca as he gulped down a coffee. Dark circles shadowed his eyes. "Your grandpa left it to you?"

"Mmm-hmm." Dominic didn't feel like discussing his business dealings with an old friend he hadn't seen in years, so he racked his brain for what to say. "How's Marchesi's doing? Still as busy as ever?"

"I almost wish it was a little less busy. I could hardly get away to come to church." Luca shook his head. "Can't complain, though."

"Well, I definitely can't complain about the biscotti. Thanks for bringing these instead of the same boring donuts."

He peered behind Luca to see Gianna, who was wearing a navy dress patterned with sunflowers and nibbling on a biscotti. "Hi, Gi-anna."

She gave him the briefest of smiles. It was enough to do strange things to his heart. "Right, you and Luca used to be friends in high school."

"Well, we *are* friends." Luca eyed the cookie in his sister's hand. "Did you get me one?"

"No, and as an older brother, I think it should have been *your* duty to bring *me* one."

Luca rolled his eyes, already marching toward the table laden with coffee and snacks. "See you later, Dom."

He lifted a hand to wave good-bye.

"So, how are you enjoying Crabtree?" Gi-anna asked.

"I'm hardly a tourist." The question rankled him, though he knew she was only making conversation.

"I'll take that as an 'I hate being back.'" She crumpled the napkin that was holding her biscotti and searched for a trash can.

"I don't *hate* it."

Her brows rose. "But, you don't love it?"

"In case you didn't know, I have plenty of reasons to have mixed feelings about my hometown." Dominic pointed to the napkin. "Here, give me that."

She passed it to him, eyebrows rising. He balled it up and tossed it in a perfect arc at the wastebasket.

"Oh, yeah. You played basketball in high school, right?" Gianna put a hand on her hip, eyeing him like she was trying to understand more than his athletic ability.

"Ten years ago, when you were…what? Sixteen?" He couldn't remember the age differences between Luca and his sisters. Though if he hadn't seen her in high school, she must have been quite a bit younger than that.

"Fourteen."

Three years. It felt like a lifetime. He inched back from her. "Right."

"Three years is such a colossal gap, isn't it?" she asked, a teasing glimmer in her brown eyes. "You can't relate to me at all, old man."

"Hey, I'm signing your paychecks now, so I would be careful about what I said if I were you, Miss Marchesi."

Her lips ticked up into a broader smile, though her expression grew serious. "Yes, but for how much longer?"

He was about to give her a witty retort to avoid thinking about his upcoming plans, when Emmett came barreling toward him and flung his arms around Dominic's mid-section. Dom ruffled his son's hair. "Ready to go, buddy?"

"Dad, I want to tell you what I did in Sunday school first."

"You can tell me in the car." He was grateful for the excuse to avoid answering Gianna. Her words pierced something in him he couldn't articulate and didn't want to.

"But Gianna is here, and I wanna tell her, too," Emmett protested.

Dominic's shoulders slumped. "I'm sure Gianna has—"

"Nowhere else to be." Gianna sat on a nearby bench and patted the space beside her. "Tell me and your dad what you did today."

Dominic sat on the other side of his son and noticed the craft he was holding. It was an Easter egg made of clay—less breakable than the real thing—and coated in a mishmash of riotous color. Though Easter had taken place over a month ago, the Sunday school teacher didn't seem to care.

He chuckled. "I see Mrs. Jenkins is still doing the same crafts."

The woman must be immortal; she'd been gray-haired with reading glasses even when she'd been teaching Dominic and Luca in Sunday school.

"Hey, I loved that egg craft," Gianna said with a laugh. "What did you paint on yours, Emmett?"

"That's me." He pointed toward a blue splotch with black on top. "And that's my dad. And that's our bookstore."

Dom squinted and made out a sloppily written sign saying Tang's. "Wow, good job, Emmett."

His heart sank, not at the thought of leaving, but disappointing his son. *Emmett will get over it.* But as he watched the animated expression on his son's face while he talked to Gianna, he was less and less sure of that.

After church, Gianna found herself strong-armed into joining Dominic and his family for lunch at the Crabtree Diner. The crab apple tree in front of it had grown over the diner's sign and obscured its original name, which was the Midnight Diner. The owners had never bothered to prune it, so it had become known as the Crabtree Diner. It was well-known for its burgers, fries and brunch food.

Dominic's parents sat on one side of the booth, while Emmett, Gianna and Dominic sat on the other, Gianna seated the closest to the wall. Emmett talked her ear off as they waited for the waitress to come to take their orders. Gianna didn't mind; she enjoyed the constant stream of chatter. It distracted her from the way Dominic was looking at her like she was about to kidnap his child. And his parents were gazing at her like they suspected... Well, she wasn't sure what. But there was *something* there that was odd.

"What can I get you guys today?" Emily Mulcair asked, popping up with a notepad. She was Thea Mulcair's sister and cut from the same gossipy cloth. At least, she had been in high school. "Oh, hey, Gianna. I didn't expect to see you here. Don't you usually eat at Marchesi's?"

The Crabtree Diner *was* one of Marchesi's competitors. Thus, Gianna didn't eat here often out of family loyalty, but she suspected Emily's comment had more to do with the people she was eating with. She would no doubt report news of their lunch together to her older sister, and soon, the entire town would be abuzz with rumors that Gianna and Dominic were an item.

"It's good to see you, too, Emily." She plucked a napkin from the holder to avoid Emily's curious gaze. Who knew that eating out could be such a harrowing experience? "I thought it would be nice to come to the diner for a change in scenery."

Dominic cleared his throat. "I'm sure the restaurant's awfully busy. We don't want to keep you away from other customers."

"I don't mind," Emily said, with a glint in her eye that suggested she was only too eager to learn more about Gianna's lunch with the Tangs.

"Emily, were you and Gianna high-school friends?" Mrs. Tang asked.

Memories surfaced of Emily making fun of her in gym class after she got smacked in the face with a volleyball and her glasses broke. Gianna tamped them down, trying not to feel like she was being bullied by the popular girls all over again. As she straightened in her seat, she reminded herself that she was *not* that insecure, shy, painfully awkward girl anymore. She was a woman who was here to get what she wanted—namely, for Dominic to stay in Crabtree and help her run the bookstore.

"Sure, we knew each other." Emily's tone

was saccharine. "We played volleyball together once."

Clearing her throat, Gianna interrupted and ordered the first thing her eyes landed on. "I'll have the breakfast poutine with peameal bacon and a chocolate milkshake."

The red vinyl booth squeaked beneath her as she shifted, leaning past Emmett and Dominic before handing the plastic-covered menu to Emily.

Dominic ordered a cheeseburger with fries for Emmett and poutine with beef short ribs for himself, rejecting his son's plea for a milkshake by pointing out that he'd eaten a caramel *and* a handful of chocolate Easter eggs. Emmett's pout in response was so adorable that it might have made Gianna give in to his request. Dominic's parents both got two eggs, toast and potatoes. She wondered what it was like to be so in sync with someone that you ordered the same meal at restaurants. Her own parents had such different tastes that they could often be found arguing over how to design a page of Marchesi's menu, let alone ordering the same foods.

"The two of you must be happy that your grandson is visiting you," Gianna said, unsure of what else to discuss and finding the topic of family to be a safe one.

"Oh, certainly. Even if he *has* almost broken a few pieces of furniture. Then again, all boys are quite rambunctious at that age, even Dominic." Olivia Tang smiled, shielding her eyes with one hand as the early afternoon sun slanted through the blinds.

Gianna chuckled. It was hard to imagine the stern, composed man sitting beside her as a rowdy young boy playing soccer or doing karate.

"Are you dating anyone, Gianna?" Mrs. Tang asked as her husband performed a magic trick involving a chocolate bar for Emmett.

Gianna felt her cheeks heat. "No, not at the moment."

"You know, your mother and I were best friends in school. It's a shame that we drifted apart after we got married at the same age… well, the same age you are now."

Gianna mustered a smile and said, "I'm sorry that you are no longer close."

"Mother," Dominic broke in. "Stop pestering poor Gianna."

"I'm only making conversation, dear. How is the bookstore doing, by the way? Dom won't tell me anything about it."

The tension in Gianna's neck increased at the introduction of an uncomfortable topic.

"You looked bored when I talked about the store, Mom." A soft smile played on Dominic's mouth despite his obvious frustration with his mother.

"Well, he won't tell me anything interesting," Mrs. Tang amended. "All he talks about is the store's finances."

"Nothing too bad, I hope." Gianna's stomach twisted itself into knots. She hadn't found any massive unpaid debts in her time as manager, but what if there was information only the owner was privy to?

"Nothing as bad as you're thinking." Dominic seemed sincere, so she let herself relax. "But there are some things I'd like to discuss with you tomorrow."

"I look forward to it." She sipped her water, looking up for any sign of Emily Mulcair. Though the restaurant was busy, the cook at the Crabtree Diner always worked at astoundingly fast speeds—though not as fast as Marchesi's—so the food should have been ready by now.

After what felt like forever, Emily came over to their booth and put down five plates. "Careful, they're hot."

She unfolded the cloth napkin and spread it over her lap, picking up her silverware as she tried to ignore the other patrons who were now looking over at their table.

"Thanks." Dominic nodded as Emily slid his poutine in front of him.

"So, Dominic, how are you liking Crabtree? Has it changed a lot since you left?" Emily asked, as though she didn't have other tables waiting for her to serve them.

"It's the same as ever," Dominic said. "In a good way."

"Well, when you left, Gianna and I were still in high school, so I guess we didn't really know you that well." Emily leaned forward, grinding fresh black pepper onto Mr. Tang's plate. "That could change now, though."

She's seriously flirting with him, right now?

"I appreciate the warm welcome," Dominic said, and his voice bore the slightest trace of sarcasm.

"Of course," Emily said, oblivious to his tone. "I'd love to hear all about your life in Toronto."

"I think some customers need a water refill," Gianna said, looking pointedly over Emily's shoulder. The waitress's glare was subtle, masked by her professionally cordial smile, but Gianna noticed it, recognizing it from the one she'd always worn in high school as she bustled away.

But before Emily left, she winked at Dominic… And was it just her imagination, or did Dominic wink back?

His parents and Emmett didn't seem to notice. Maybe it was all in her head?

Gianna sighed, bowing her head over her plate in silent prayer as the Tangs did the same.

They all dug into their food and were silent for a few moments. Dominic blinked rapidly and rubbed his eye. "There's something in my contact lens. I'll be right back."

Dominic's parents began eating, commenting on how delicious the food was—though Olivia Tang mentioned that it couldn't compare to Marchesi's—and Emmett asked if he could have a sip of Gianna's chocolate shake. Gianna gave Emmett an extra straw so he could try it, but she reminded him that Dominic hadn't let him order his own for a reason. His grandpa chimed in, though Mr. Tang's tone was more gentle than scolding as he told his grandson not to steal too much of Gianna's drink.

"Is *everyone* in Crabtree so gossipy, or

did I just forget how quickly rumors spread around here?" Dominic shook his head as he slid back into the booth next to Emmett, who was now sandwiched between them. "I was stopped three times on my way back from the bathroom by people asking me questions about Emmett."

She was grateful for the change in subject, since she wasn't sure how he would feel about her letting Emmett have a sip of her milkshake. Though she agreed that the Mulcair sisters weren't the friendliest people in Crabtree, the urge to defend her hometown surged in her chest. "They're not *gossipy*. There's just not a lot to talk about here."

"Everyone in town seems to have taken it upon themselves to be part of my personal welcoming committee." He took a sip of water.

"And you don't feel welcome?" she said, arching an eyebrow.

"I feel more at home in the bookstore than I did just now."

Gianna hid her smile of victory at his confession as she bit into a french fry. "Good to know."

She would eat her delicious poutine, get through this lunch and come up with a plan to

make Dominic love the bookstore and Crabtree so much that he never wanted to leave.
   How hard could that be?

Chapter Five

The following Monday marked two weeks since Dominic had first arrived in Crabtree. He'd talked to Gianna about the uneasy financial shape the store was in—something she seemed to accept with a brisk nod and a stiff upper lip. Philip Tang had been a generous employer and had given abundantly to his employees, sometimes too much, but Gianna seemed more pragmatic than that. Despite her idealistic notions, she seemed to have a practical nature.

Though he'd been dreading the visit, he was surprised to find that he didn't mind being back in town. He enjoyed working at the bookstore. Dominic had been filing receipts, looking through financial reports and doing other bookkeeping-related things, which were not his favorite, even if he *was* an accountant by trade.

Throughout his workday, he would come out of the back office and see Gianna making conversation with the customers or reading to the children during the daily reading hour hosted by Tang's. Sometimes he would run the store while she left to get a coffee from the café down the street, or he would stretch his legs and go get a biscotti from Marchesi's, bringing back an egg tart for Gianna. He'd learned that they were her favorite from the vast selection of delicious Italian and Chinese pastries available at her family's restaurant.

Today, however, just as he was returning from one of these culinary quests, his son called out to him. "Dad!"

Emmett had been splitting his time between reading in the bookstore and spending time with his grandparents, who had taken him swimming, hiking and even to Olivia's knitting group. Today, he was at the bookstore.

"What's up, buddy?" He handed Gianna an Americano from Marchesi's, then downed his espresso and walked toward his son, who was in the children's reading corner.

"We're reading *The BFG* for the reading hour today, but Gianna said she's not good at doing all the voices. Can you read it for us? Please?" Emmett's wide, pleading eyes made him automatically extend a hand to take the proffered book from his son.

"*The BFG*? Isn't this book a little too long for a reading hour?" he asked, his gaze turning to Gianna, who was sipping her coffee.

"We'll be reading it all month for the middle schoolers. They chose the genre for the month of June," Gianna said, pointing at a whiteboard where the word *fantasy* was written in swirling blue letters. "Then I picked the book. I read it when I was a bit older than Emmett."

Emmett was at an advanced reading level for his age, devouring books at such a speed that the librarians knew him by name.

"As did I, for Mrs. Hoffman's class," he recalled.

"I'm surprised you remember," she teased, with a twinkle in her eyes. That sparkle faded a moment later, though, for reasons he couldn't fathom.

After all, for all intents and purposes, Gianna Marchesi was simply an employee. Her private thoughts were of no concern to him.

She assembled the various children into a circle in the back corner of the store and directed Dominic to sit in the rocking chair. As he started reading, he yearned to lose himself in the story of Sophie and the giant and various made-up words. However, he found his attention diverted by one of the children giggling, or Gianna, who was standing in the corner, watching him read. Occasionally, one of the children would stop him to ask a question, and he would feel her gaze on him as he answered. Finally, when the hour was up, he stood, his eyes locking on Gianna's. He crossed the room and passed the book to her.

Her fingers brushed his as she took the book from him. Instead of reshelving it, she rocked back on her heels. "You did a great job with the kids today. Not everyone can get them to sit still and listen for an hour, especially without screens involved."

Gianna's brown eyes were warm, and her praise seemed sincere. Her smile reached into his chest and warmed places that he hadn't realized were cold.

"Thank you." He wasn't sure why her approval mattered so much to him.

They fell silent, listening to the chatter of children as their parents came to pick them up.

Just then, he heard a familiar voice. He spun around to see Luca.

"Dom," Luca said. "Long time no see."

"We just saw each other on Sunday." Like most members of his family, Luca had a rather gregarious personality. In high school, it had made it easier for Dominic, quiet and gawky at six foot two, to fall into his shadow. He'd always preferred to be in the background instead of the spotlight.

"Well, I had to stop by and see if you were treating my sister all right," Luca said. "I hope you're not being too hard on her. I know she has that annoying habit of licking her finger when she turns the pages of a book, but—"

"Hey!" Gianna stepped back from Dominic and toward her brother. "I only do that with my own books, not the ones in the store."

"So, you love reading, and you're surrounded by books all the time, but you never read them?" Lucas shook his head. "Tell me another lie."

Gianna rolled her eyes. "I'm a professional. You, on the other hand, once stole a bread stick off someone's plate in the middle of your shift."

Dominic cleared his throat, uncomfortable with the siblings' bickering. As an only child, he'd never had anyone to argue with. Emmett would likely never have siblings, either. The thought pained him more than he wanted to admit. "Well, if that's all you came here for,

Luca, I'm going to head to the office and finish up some work."

"No, wait. I wanted to ask you to shoot
some hoops with me, just like old times. Your
son can come, too, and I'll even bring my
cousin Pietro. They're about the same age."

Dom looked over at Emmett, who was
lying upside down on a beanbag chair in
the kids' corner, reading a new comic book.
"Emmett, you're going to ruin your eyes reading like that. Sit up straight."

Groaning, his son set down the book and
did a backflip to get into an upright position.
Crash!

All three adults watched in horror as the
shelf behind him toppled over...hitting the
one behind it...and knocking over yet another
shelf. Books tumbled to the ground around
the boy. Dust rose in small clouds, tickling
the back of Dominic's throat.

"Ouch." Emmett's eyes were wide as he
scanned the store.

"Well," Gianna said after a moment, her
voice strained. "I'm glad this happened after
the children's reading hour."

Dominic alternated between scolding his
son and asking him a thousand questions to

ensure Emmett wasn't hurt, before assessing the damage to the store.

Gianna wanted to investigate, but as soon as she had taken a few steps toward the mess, Dominic shot her a look rather like the one he had given Emmett. "These platforms that the shelves are on look dangerous and unstable. I don't want anyone to get hurt."

"But it's okay for you to get hurt?" she said, folding her arms over her chest.

His brows furrowed. "As you've made clear, Miss Marchesi, I own the store now—"

"So you know precisely where to reshelve all of these books that have fallen down?" Gianna asked. Luca snickered from behind her; she'd forgotten he was still there amid the chaos.

Dominic didn't respond, the stubborn set of his jaw giving her all the answers she needed. He rubbed his face, drawing her eyes to his rolled-up sleeves. Gianna was annoyed with herself for noticing how strong his forearms looked while the bookstore was such a mess. *Get a hold of yourself.* Besides, what if he was still heartbroken over his ex? Perhaps he'd sworn off dating forever. She couldn't blame him if that was the case.

"I'm sorry, Gianna," Emmett said, running up and flinging himself at her in a hug. "I didn't mean to mess things up with the books...and everything."

She patted him on the head, not expecting the sudden embrace. "It's not your fault, but next time you try to be a stuntman, please do it outside the store."

He nodded emphatically, a lock of dark hair flopping over his forehead. The boy was adorable; he must have gotten his looks from his father.

"Okay," he said, sniffling. "I'm still sorry, though. Is Tang's going to be okay? Am I going to get in trouble?"

"You'll have to ask your dad about that," she said, fighting a smile at his expression. He looked so upset over the damage to the books, his lower lip quivering in a pout, that it warmed her heart.

Dominic cleared his throat again. Was he having an allergic reaction to the dust? "Emmett, we're going to stay here with Gianna and figure out how best to clean this up. You're going to help, right?"

Emmett nodded again, his lower lip wobbling. He clutched the hem of her shirt even as he turned to face his dad. "Are you mad at me?"

"No, but as Gianna said, I don't want you to do any more tricks like that when you're indoors, okay? It's dangerous for you and the people around you." Emmett released her shirt to take Dominic's hand.

The man was good with children. She supposed that shouldn't have come as a surprise, considering he had a seven-year-old son, but there were some fathers who were terrible at parenting and still more men who would rather shirk their duties than spend time with their kids. Dominic was different. He had genuinely seemed to enjoy reading to the middle schoolers today, and he hadn't minded when they had interrupted his reading of *The BFG* to ask what *snozzcumbers* tasted like.

Luca elbowed her. "G, you're staring."

"What? No, I'm not," she said reflexively, annoyed by her older brother's insinuation.

"He has a kid, Gianna, and you're…too young for that," he said.

She gritted her teeth, tired of the constant assumptions from her family that just because she hadn't chosen to go into the family business, she was somehow less responsible or less competent than they were. "He's my boss. And he might not even stick around Crabtree. I'm not stupid, Luca."

He looked around the mess that had been made of her displays of hand-painted books. All her hard work was scattered on the floor. His tone softened. "It's just… I heard you had lunch with him and his parents."

Gianna fiddled with the end of her braid. "It wasn't a date or anything."

"No, but it seems a bit too friendly for you to be with a guy who's your boss."

"It was just professional."

Her annoyed tone must have caused him to stop harping on the subject. "Do you want me to stick around and help clean up?"

She glanced at her watch; it was going to be the dinner rush at Marchesi's soon. "No, go. Dominic and I have this under control."

Luca hugged her, fist-bumped Dominic and Emmett with promises of a pickup basketball game later that week and then left. With her hands on her hips, Gianna looked around the place. Her heart was heavy at the thought that Dominic might be counting this incident as yet another mark against the store. Against her.

Instead of looking smug, he just turned to her expectantly. "Where do you keep the dustpan? I'm going to clean up the broken glass."

"I'll go get it for you." As she walked toward the broom closet, Gianna sighed.

She'd misjudged him. She was beginning to realize she had a bad habit of doing that.

Dominic yawned, his back aching as his stomach grumbled. He and Gianna had spent the better part of an hour cleaning up the shattered remains of broken glass, and then he'd spent another thirty minutes righting the shelves. The shelves hadn't simply fallen over. They'd also broken lamps, crushed the strings of lights that had been strung over them and smashed into the AC unit, meaning that would need to be fixed to the tune of a thousand dollars, and soon, since it was the beginning of summer. On top of that, the bookshelves had also knocked over a low-hanging ceiling lamp, which had shattered and pulled down some water-damaged ceiling tiles with it. This would be even more of a burden on the store's already strained budget, meaning that they would *definitely* need to win in one of the categories of the town's annual fair if they wanted any hope of getting their ledger out of the red.

And that was all on top of the fact that he still didn't have a job waiting for him back in Toronto. His job-hunting had been to no avail so far.

Dominic began to have second thoughts about taking on the responsibility of the bookstore as he stretched his tired muscles. Thankfully, the shelves hadn't been too heavy to lift after the books had all tumbled out of them. Not wanting to be left on the sidelines, Emmett was assigned the task of gathering all the books into neat piles, once they had ensured that there was no broken glass on any of the volumes.

A pang of guilt racked him every time he looked at the state of disarray that the bookstore was in. Sure, he hadn't wanted to keep it when he'd first returned to Crabtree, but that didn't mean he wanted the store to be completely wrecked. His son was his responsibility, and he should've made it clearer to Emmett that he shouldn't do backflips indoors. Did the accident make him a bad father? One who allowed his son to run rampant, causing problems wherever he went?

He'd long told himself that if Carly didn't want—or need—him and Emmett, then neither of them needed her. However, that didn't mean Emmett could do without a motherly, civilizing presence in his life. He chewed on his lower lip, a headache throbbing at his temples as he thought about what he would have to do to make this store functional again. More importantly, what he would have to do to make sure his son didn't repeat this sort of incident in the future.

As the three of them sorted, stacked and organized the store's books, fixtures and bookish knickknacks, the two of them made note of what needed to be replaced, repaired or thrown away. Dominic was surprised to see some books that stood out from the others. Tang's sold a mix of new and used, paperbacks and hardcovers, but he had never seen anything like the one in his hands right now.

"Is this a special edition?" he asked Gianna as Emmett got up to stretch his legs. The book was a fantasy romance he didn't recognize, with the edges painted a deep blue, sprinkled with glittering stars, showing two lovers silhouetted against the backdrop. "Because if it is, I'm sorry it was caught up in this mess—"

"No, no," Gianna said, shaking her head. "You don't need to apologize. I know how much of a handful young boys can be. Luca was even worse growing up. Also, I guess that is kind of a special edition… I painted it myself."

"Wow." He looked down at the cover, which he could see now had been repainted as well, and traced his fingers over the beautiful brushstrokes. "Gianna, this…it's a masterpiece."

"It's just a hobby," she said quickly, reaching for the book and setting it gently into a box next to her. "Nothing special."

"Gianna, you could totally sell these."

She shrugged at him, smiling as a shaft of late afternoon sunlight slid through the window and illuminated her face. She was beautiful and vivacious and everything he wanted but couldn't let himself have.

Emmett came back from his walk with a rolling cart with shelves. "Can we put the books on this?"

"Of course," Gianna said, jumping to her feet. "Here, I'll show you how to sort them on the rack. I think we're almost finished, and then you and your dad can go home and eat dinner, okay? I think I heard *someone's* stomach grumbling earlier."

Emmett chuckled as he helped Gianna put the books away. "That was probably my dad."

Dominic was surprised at the way the back of his neck heated from the comment. "What do you want for dinner, Emmett?"

"Marchesi's!" Emmett exclaimed.

"Only two weeks here, and he's already obsessed with the baked risotto," Dominic said as he picked up a stack of books and carried them over to the cart. As he set them down, he saw the look on Gianna's face. It was one of... annoyance? Discomfort? "Are you okay?"

His hand brushed against hers as he arranged the books on the cart's top shelf, and he couldn't help but notice how much smaller her hand was compared to his. Gianna brushed her hair so that it fell over her face, hiding her expression from him. She seemed...vulnerable. Not just physically, but emotionally, like he'd probed a tender spot, and she was retreating back into her shell. He hadn't thought she was shy, since she seemed so much more outgoing than he was.

"I'm fine. I'm glad he likes the food." She wrung her hands, the gesture belying her cheery tone. "That's great."

He tried to understand her. She had gone straight to the restaurant after finding out he wanted to gut the bookstore, so it couldn't be that she hated it. Was there something else about the family business that bothered her? Did she simply hate baked risotto?

"Dad, I finished stacking all the books in

my pile. Are you done yet?" Emmett fidgeted with his hands before stuffing them into
his pockets, clearly being cautious of breaking anything else in the store, yet still full of
rambunctious energy as always.

Gianna straightened, her expression stiff-
ening into a polite mask. "You two can go. I'll
just put this cart in the supply room and lock
up. We'll have to come in early tomorrow to
see what should be done about the ceiling
tiles, though. Thanks again for all your help."

He wanted to stay and ask her why she
was acting like a stranger, but then again, she
practically was one. What business was it of
his, even if the sight of her looking so distant
sent a strange sensation through him?

Chapter Six

Before the summer sun rose above the bluish-gray outline of the Rockies, Dominic met Luca in front of Tang's, fumbling with his keys for a moment before he could open the door. The bookstore wouldn't open for another three hours, but he'd figured he would get a head start. He'd barely been able to sleep last night, too preoccupied by thoughts of how he'd be able to pay for all the damage one moment of careless parenting had wreaked.

"Thanks again for agreeing to help me clean the rest of this. Emmett wanted to come, but I didn't want him to get hurt." Dominic put his keys away, not looking at his old friend. A part of him was embarrassed that this situation had happened in the first place, that he'd allowed himself to be distracted enough to let his son destroy much of the bookstore with one backflip. "I know you wanted to play basketball instead, but—"

"No worries." Luca whistled as he flipped on the light switch. "Wow, Emmett really did a number on this place, no offense."

"None taken." In the light of the dawning sun, with the harsh fluorescents flipped on and buzzing overhead, the bookstore's chaos was thrown into stark relief. The bookshelves had been righted and the books put away on carts—well, most of them—but the small space, which had once looked so cozy and inviting, now resembled a pigsty. Broken light bulbs glinted in the white sunlight and old ceiling tiles were scattered across the navy carpet.

"I guess we'd better start vacuuming." Dominic retrieved the cleaning supplies from the back, and they began to work in silence.

Just as Dominic turned off the vacuum after cleaning the carpet, Luca spoke. "How have you been these past seven years, Dom? I know the breakup was hard on you, but it's been for the best, right?"

Had it been for the best? At the time, his emotions had been so raw and confused that he'd had no idea what to think, only feeling as if he'd hit rock bottom. But it was there, in the worst possible state, that God had found him. That was worth something.

If only he could decide what to do with this bookstore.

"You could say that, yeah." He shrugged. "What about you? It's been seven years. Any girl in your life?"

Luca emptied his dustpan into the garbage. "Nah, I'm too young to settle down. Too much going on at the restaurant for me to think about that right now, at least."

Growing up, Dominic had always wondered what it would be like to be Luca Marchesi. To know exactly what your place was in the world and to be born into a role that had been decided for you from birth. Luca had always known his path. Dominic had never wanted to become an engineer like his father, and while he made a living as an accountant, it wasn't the kind of work he relished.

"Business is doing pretty well. Looks like all of Crabtree still loves Marchesi's, even if they *did* open up that diner."

Luca coughed as a puff of dust rose up, and he swatted it away. "It would be nice if G would come back to work for us. We're pretty swamped, especially on the weekends."

The thought of Gianna leaving to work at Marchesi's sparked a sudden—well, he couldn't quite describe the feeling. Possessiveness. Jealousy. Gianna had said she wasn't interested in working for her family restaurant before, so why was he so worried? "She's mi—I mean, my employee. You're not allowed to poach her."

Luca chuckled, clapping him on the back. "Lighten up, Dominic. I was just saying, it'd be nice to have more help at the restaurant."

They lapsed back into a tense silence for a few moments, neither sure what to say, as Dominic threw away the broken ceiling tiles and Luca carefully disassembled what remained of the ceiling lamp. Just as they had finished cleaning, the sun finished its ascent across the sky, hovering above the horizon. Luca opened and closed his mouth, seeming to think better of what he wanted to say as he headed for the door.

Dominic put away his tools. "If something's bothering you, Luca, just spit it out. I'm not going to be offended."

"I didn't say I was mad." Luca rubbed a spot of plaster off his cheek.

"Just say it."

"I don't want you hanging around my sister, Dom."

He snorted reflexively. "Nothing's happening between me and Gianna."

"Oh, yeah?" One of Luca's eyebrows arched. "Prove it."

"You want me to prove something that doesn't exist?"

Sure, Gianna was pretty and kind and bright and great with Emmett, and she… Well, she was a good person. But noticing those things about her meant he *did* like her in the way that Luca was talking about.

Luca folded his arms across his chest. "I don't want you to get her attached to you and then just pick up and leave. We all know you won't be sticking around Crabtree for long."

"We're just friends," Dominic said. "Barely. We just work together."

"Okay, fine. But don't mess with Gianna's head by making her think you're gonna stay here when you're planning to run back to Toronto."

Dominic disliked the way Luca said "run back to Toronto," as though he'd left Crabtree all those years ago to escape his problems. He hadn't. He'd had every reason to leave town, not merely because of Carly or the scandal. Dominic had had a solid accounting job in Toronto and a predictable life. He was going back there…eventually. Yet the longer he was here, the less Toronto felt like real life, and the more Crabtree did.

Luca went on. "I'm sure you have your life all under control. Just warning you, though. Stay away from my sister."

"I'll take it under advisement." Then he held the front door open for his high-school friend, hinting that he was no longer needed in the store. "Just remember, she *chose* to stay in the bookstore and work here when I wanted to gut the place. I didn't force her to do any of this."

"How was your lunch with Dominic?" Estella said the moment Gianna walked into their mother's garden.

Every week, the Marchesi siblings were strongly encouraged—required—to help out in the family garden. The backyard oasis contained tomato vines, carrots, garlic, onions, an assortment of hardy perennials and a patch of dandelions that their mother used for tea. They were all used in the restaurant or in their parents' home cooking. As Marchesi siblings, their responsibilities included watering the plants, clearing out any weeds that were *not* dandelions and mowing the lawn.

"It's not like we had a date or anything. We were with his parents and Emmett."

"I wouldn't have asked you if you would've just told me."

She'd spent that Sunday afternoon reading and napping on the back porch. No one could dissuade her from this usual routine, and no one dared to try. Gianna was uncharacteristically cranky without her naps, something that her mother joked she had never grown out of.

"It was fine." She tied her wavy brown hair back into a high ponytail, putting it through one of her mother's old sun visors, and pulled on her usual cheery yellow gardening gloves, patterned with light blue dots. "Can we get started now?"

"Not until you tell me something more substantial than *fine*." Estella pulled the lawn mower out of the gardening shed and began pushing it through the backyard grass, which had grown high thanks to the unseasonably heavy rains this May.

Gianna began tugging at a tenacious dandelion root that had nestled between the flower bed and the tomato vines, digging at it with a screwdriver. "His mother asked me if I was seeing anyone."

Estella squealed. "So, she wants you to date her son!"

"No, I'm pretty sure that was the last thing on her mind." Unless… Estella was right.

"So, *are* you?" Estella asked, grunting as the lawn mower got stuck on a pine cone. She bent down to pick it up and threw it over her shoulder.

"Am I what?" Gianna gave another yank, and the stem of the weed broke off, leaving the root buried deep in the soil. *Ugh*. She knelt on an old knee pad her mother kept in the garden to dig it out.

"Are you seeing anyone?"

Growing up, Estella and Lillian, Gianna's best friend, had always banded together against Gianna, being the more boy-crazy members of Gianna's immediate circle. The two of them would check out romance novels from the library, swooning and sighing and devising plans to catch the eye of the cute guy who worked at the movie theater so he would let them in for free (it worked until the cinema's manager found out). They didn't understand Gianna's preference for thrillers and mystery books, which seemed more realistic to her. Crimes happened more often than people falling—and staying—in love.

"I'm not. You would probably know about it before I did." Gianna burrowed the screwdriver deeper into the dirt and finally got the root out. She blew out a long breath, trying to get a few wisps of hair out of her face as she dumped the weed into a nearby wicker basket to be composted later.

"You're so secretive, Gianna. I doubt that would be the case." Estella pushed the mower across another row of grass. "You *never* tell us anything."

Because you would be the first to tell everybody about it. She didn't say that out loud, though. She knew her younger sister just wanted to connect with her. But Gianna was too reserved—and if that made her secretive, so what?—to tell everything to Estella.

"I don't think that's true. I told you guys when Dominic Tang came into town."

"You never tell us anything *personal*," Estella amended.

You never listen, anyway. She bit her tongue, not wanting to turn a day of gardening into a heated fight with her sister. "I'll try to be better about it."

"I just wish you would open up more."

Estella sighed. "Ever since you decided you didn't want to work at Marchesi's, it's like you're drifting away."

Gianna's brows knit together. Was that true? Did her family feel like she had abandoned them for the bookstore?

"I'm still here on Saturday nights for dinner," she offered up weakly. "I'm always going to be a Marchesi."

"I know, but...it feels like you chose the bookstore over us." Estella finished pushing the mower through the last row of grass and began hauling it back toward the shed.

She began tugging up another weed. "I just wanted my own thing. The restaurant and you guys are still important to me. I just didn't... didn't want to work at Marchesi's my whole life."

"Why not?" Estella said, raking up the cut grass into neat piles.

"Because..." She sighed. "I guess I didn't want to do what everyone else expected of me. There's nothing wrong with Marchesi's. You know I love it. I...just didn't belong there."

"But you're a Marchesi." Estella's voice was tender despite her stiff, jerky movements as she raked the grass. "If you don't belong there, where do you belong?"

It was a question she'd been asking herself far too often.

Then Estella asked, "If Dominic Tang sells the bookstore or guts it, what are you going to do?"

Gianna flinched at the mention of gutting the bookstore like Estella had suggested chopping off one of her limbs. "Go back to Marchesi's, just like Dad wants."

And that was what scared her the most.

Chapter Seven

Although the bookstore was still in a state of limbo, with Dominic making promises that didn't allay her fears, Gianna needed to focus on the event of the season: Crabtree's annual fair. It was always the town's biggest celebration, aside from their Christmas parade, with a midway, various carnival foods and displays of local businesses' wares. Gianna looked forward to sampling the various baked goods and treats every year. This year, however, if she didn't convince Dominic that the store was a good investment before the fair, she'd have to go back to working at the restaurant. And that prospect was looming heavier over her head the closer they got to the fair.

She tried not to think about Dominic's words to her before they'd closed up the store last night. They had been something like "I'll figure something out" when she asked him about the damaged ceiling tiles, broken AC unit, mangled water pipe and books that would need to be replaced. Then there would be the lost revenue from however long it would take them to replace and repair everything. Just thinking about that made her chest ache.

Even after he and Luca had come in early this morning to help further clean up the store, it wouldn't be enough until they paid for all the replacements and repairs.

This crisis felt like an echo of the taunts that had been thrown at her by her high-school bullies or her own parents' patronizing words. *You'll never make it. Just give up and go home. Why don't you stick to something safer?* Just as she'd thought the bookstore might become a town staple, it was hit with another fire to put out.

Dominic Tang was coming dangerously close to ruining her life, even if his son was adorable and he was infuriatingly attractive.

So here she was, on a Tuesday morning, trying to ignore the remnants of Emmett's incident. Dominic had helped clean up yesterday and this morning, but she still couldn't help but notice the missing ceiling tiles or the broken AC unit. Gianna had turned Tang's into a safe haven, and she wanted it to be restored to that state. Unfortunately, Crabtree was such a small town that there was only one repairperson who could fix the AC unit, and he was out of town. According to his wife, he wouldn't be back for a few weeks.

She began preparing her workspace to decorate books for the fair. As she did an inventory of the materials she kept for spraying and painting the fore edges of books, the front doorbell jingled. She didn't look up from organizing her workspace. "Dominic, did you bring me a coffee?"

He often came in around this time with an Americano from her family's restaurant or one of their fabulous espressos, and she had come to expect—even anticipate—the drink *and* his company. Though, she hadn't expected him to help her with *this*.

"No, just your best friend," said Lillian Cheng as she bounded into the store with a bag of art supplies. Gianna was grateful that her best friend had taken time off from her budding wedding-planning business to come help her. She worked closely with the town's florist, Alicia Baker, who owned Blooming

Bouquets, the shop that supplied Gianna with the flowers she liked to decorate Tang's with. "You didn't mention that Dominic Tang was good-looking *and* a supplier of free coffee, too, Gianna. If I had known, I would have snatched him up the moment he walked into Marchesi's."

"Lil, please," she said with a laugh. "All you know about him is that he's handsome and sometimes buys me coffee, and you want to date him?"

"I hear he's also good with kids. Besides, Crabtree is so small, he might as well be new to town," Lillian said, setting down her bag of brushes, paints and who knew what else next to her on the table. "Though the town *does* have a long memory."

Gianna chewed on her lower lip as she looked at the book in front of her. *Pride and Prejudice.* "Come on, *Lillian,* enough guy talk. Let's focus on the project."

Lillian's expression soured at the sound of her full name, which only her mother called her.

"You're entering this into the annual fair, right? What's the theme this year?" Lillian took out her tools, placing them on the table next to the books.

"Your mom coordinates the fair every year. Don't you know?"

Lillian dropped a paintbrush. "That was a test. The theme of the fair is *love*."

Lil loved love (the name of her wedding business was Love Designed by Lillian) and anything romance related. Gianna looked down at the books spread out on the table. Besides *Pride and Prejudice*, there were some popular romance novels, a book on love languages, C. S. Lewis's *The Four Loves* and a few others. Gianna had forgotten about the fair and its theme with all the excitement that had happened since she had first gathered the books to be painted. Especially after the bookstore had been…unexpectedly rearranged.

"Right, it completely slipped my mind." Her phone dinged. It was Dominic.

"Ooh, is that him?" Lillian snatched up her phone before she could even reach for it. "I won't text him anything, I swear!"

Gianna sighed. "The last time you said that, we were in high school, and you asked out the captain of the basketball team on my behalf. But he was too terrified of my brother to even think about saying yes, not to mention that he thought I was Estella."

"So it all worked out in the end!" her best friend insisted.

"Lil, he told Luca! And then Luca lectured me for half an hour about talking to guys," she said with a groan. "What does the text say?"

"'Dear Gianna, I'd like to confess my undying love and ask you to be the stepmother to my son—'"

"No, Lillian, the *real* text," she said with an eye roll.

Lillian's antics had always made life more interesting—if not more dramatic. However, the idea that Gianna would ever date Dominic was preposterous. His past in Crabtree shrouded him in scandal. That was the last thing Gianna wanted. If she was going to stand out in the town, it wouldn't be for notoriety.

Plus, Dominic had a son. Was she ready to even consider being a stepmother or any kind of parent? Watching Emmett while he was in the store was one thing. Helping to raise a child was another.

"Gianna, you zoned out on me." Lillian snapped her fingers inches from her nose, causing Gianna to stumble back and grip the tabletop to keep her balance. "Are you okay?"

Dominic had asked her the same question when they'd been cleaning up the store. He was uncannily perceptive of her emotions, or maybe she just wore them too blatantly across her face. "I'm fine."

"You were considering the idea of dating Dominic, weren't you?"

"No," she said, not wanting to hear Lillian's smug boasting.

"Okay, then. In that case, let me read his real text to you. 'I'm not coming into the store today, as Emmett and I are going on a family outing with my parents. I apologize for the late notice, but it is my mom's birthday today. I hope you can understand.' Wow, Gianna, he's so formal. Are you sure he's Luca's age? He texts like an eighty-year-old."

"Eighty-year-olds don't text," she said automatically. "Tell him it's fine. It's not like I'm his boss."

Why did she feel so disappointed at the prospect of not seeing him today? It was probably because she'd gotten used to his presence in the store over the past few weeks, and now she couldn't quite picture the store without his and Emmett's presence. Dominic working on the accounts in the back office or bringing her coffee or sharing a pastry from

Marchesi's with her. Talking to him had become a habit to her. He was now a fixture of Tang's, just as much as the bookshelves or the cozy chairs or the smell of old books were.

And that was the problem. There was no guarantee that his stay would be permanent.

"Done." Lillian spread a tarp over their work surface and cracked open a window to keep the smell of paint from overwhelming them. "Now, it's time we get to work."

They began painting the edges of the books, first spraying them with a base coating, then adding finer details. Lillian suggested how to decorate each volume according to its plot and genre, and Gianna tried to absorb herself in her work, but she soon realized…she almost *missed* having Dominic Tang at the store. It had been kind—more than kind— of him to say that he thought she should sell the books. That he thought they were beautiful. Worth more than a frivolous hobby to just while away her time with.

He'd complimented her art, and it meant a lot to her. Perhaps more than it ought to.

She'd spent all her life hearing from her parents and her siblings that her dream of being an artist was unrealistic, that she should stick to business, or better yet, stick to the *family* business. While she enjoyed cooking and knew the basics of all her parents' recipes, she'd always wanted something else. Gianna wanted to stand out. She wanted a career of her own, something that would set her apart from the family.

Yet even as she fought Dominic Tang to keep the bookstore alive, she wondered why she was doing it. It couldn't just be that it was the only job she'd ever known and cared so deeply for. Gianna felt like she wasn't so much a creature of habit that she couldn't pick up and find another job.

No, deep down the bookstore was a part of her, and she knew it. Leaving the bookstore would be like leaving a piece of herself —her creativity and her passion and her heart—behind.

"Gianna, you're getting paint all over your clothes," Lillian said.

She looked down at her white T-shirt. "Oh, no. I guess I shouldn't have worn white, huh?"

Or started thinking that maybe, just maybe, Dominic Tang might be her ideal man.

After his mother's birthday dinner, which he and Emmett had labored over for three hours—the stir-fry was a simple dish, but Emmett's help doubled the amount of time necessary to make it—Dominic sat on the couch and tried to relax. He was between his father and his son, both of whom were engrossed in playing the video game *Mario Kart*. However, as he tried to focus on the TV, his mind wandered back to the bookstore. He wondered what Gianna had done at the store that day and worried about how much of the store's emergency fund they'd need to make the repairs.

He'd prayed about the store numerous times, wondering if he was making the right decision. If he was honoring God by honoring his grandfather's wishes. And still, after countless hours of prayer, he felt no closer to an answer. All he knew was that Emmett's face lit up every time he walked into the store. He loved spending time there and having Gianna treat him like her little assistant who shelved books for her. The other employee who worked there, Garrett, treated Emmett like a little brother.

His son's happiness was one thing. But what about providing for Emmett's future? The bookstore had been a risky venture to begin with, and now with all the renovations and repairs that would need to be done?

"Dominic, honey, could you drive me to

Cecilia Cheng's house? You know I don't like driving after dark, and your father doesn't, either," his mother said.

"Sure thing," he said. "Emmett, do you want to come?"

His son just barely shook his head, not looking up from the screen, which showed a rainbow-colored course that his car was barreling down. Dominic chuckled, mussed his son's hair and grabbed his keys.

"So, why are you going over to Auntie Cecilia's house at this hour with… Is that a pie?" he asked his mom as they pulled out of the driveway. She carried a foil-covered dish, which smelled delicious.

"No, but it is a dessert. It's for the annual fair. I wanted to let her taste-test it before I submitted it to the competition," she said. "It's always good to have a second opinion on these things."

The annual fair. In all the hubbub of the shelves toppling over, he'd nearly forgotten about his promise to stay in Crabtree until the annual fair. "What's the theme this year?"

"It's *love*," his mother said, with a tad more emphasis than he would have liked.

"Why are you saying the word *love* like that?" he asked, wary of the answer.

"No reason, honey. If you're reading more into it than there is, I'm beginning to think you have some preoccupation with love."

He couldn't help but feel like his mother had maneuvered him into a corner. "What kind of dessert did you make?"

"I'll tell you when you respond properly to my statement. Don't try to change the subject, mister."

The aroma was mouthwatering. "Is it apple pie?"

"No. Dom, when are you going to find a nice girl and fall in love?" his mother said, abandoning her indirect tactics for a less subtle strategy. "You know your father and I worry about you and Emmett being all alone in the big city—"

"We have God and each other," he said. "I don't need anyone else. Besides, I can't just date any girl. She would have to be a good mother to Emmett, and there aren't many women willing to take on another woman's child."

"So you admit that you *have* thought about dating someone." The foil covering the pie dish crinkled, and his stomach growled. "It's Chinese."

"What?"

He came to a halt at a stop sign to let a couple go by. They were pushing a stroller and holding a little girl's hand, and the sight made his heart twinge.

"I said the dessert is Chinese. That's your only hint," his mother said. "Tell me about the perfect woman, then. The only one who could tempt you to date again."

He sighed, knowing his mother would never stop bringing up the topic until he gave in. "First, she should be good with children."

Unbidden, the memory of Gianna talking to Emmett gently but firmly on the day of the bookstore incident flashed into his mind. Gianna was too young for him, too closely tied to Crabtree, when he wanted the opposite.

"Go on."

"She should know how to cook, though she doesn't necessarily have to be great at it."

"That goes without saying," his mother scoffed.

He tried to hide his laugh. After all his years away, Dominic had nearly forgotten how old-fashioned his mother was. He went on. "She should be loving and kind, but not afraid to stand her ground and put up a fight when it's called for."

One picture came to mind and wouldn't

leave: Gianna talking back to him when she'd taken their drink orders during his first visit to Marchesi's in years.

"Well, you need someone who can handle your stubbornness," his mother said with a knowing look.

"I'm not stubborn," he protested.

"Yes, you are. I never thought you would come back home, even after your grandfather left you the bookstore," she said with a wry smile. "I'm glad you returned, though."

"I'm glad I'm back, too," he said, surprised to find that he meant it.

Dominic parked in front of Cecilia Cheng's house and opened the door for his mother. She thanked him as he took the pie dish from her.

"Egg tarts," he said after peeking under the foil when she wasn't looking.

"You would be correct," she said as they marched up the steps to the Chengs' front porch, which was half obscured by a Douglas fir planted in the front yard and bathed in the warm glow of Christmas lights even in the middle of June.

"Olivia, it's so lovely to see you! And Dominic, look at you! You're all grown up," Cecilia said, welcoming them into the cozy bungalow. "Bryan, come here! The Tangs are here, and they've brought dessert."

"That will summon any man in five seconds," his mother said with a chuckle as they took off their shoes and left them on a mat in the foyer.

He would've contradicted her, but found he had no leg to stand on when it came to his mother's cooking. "I won't deny that."

"Come in, you two, come into the dining room." Cecilia motioned them forward. "Ah, there's my husband now."

Bryan Cheng, a perpetually slim man— despite being a regular at Marchesi's—with thinning gray hair and a jolly laugh, entered the dining room. "Dominic! I remember when you were a young boy, riding bicycles across my lawn with Luca. Now you're a grown man with a son of your own. How time flies!"

"It sure does, Uncle," he said, stepping forward to shake the man's hand. Something about the way Bryan mentioned the past felt less stifling than expected; he still saw how Dominic's childhood had been, and he also saw the man he'd become.

"I can't wait to try this," Cecilia said, grabbing silverware and plates from the kitchen. "Dominic, I saw the lovely project that Gianna says she's thinking of entering into the fair. Truly beautiful work—you should be glad that she's representing your store."

"What project, Auntie?"

"Oh, those beautiful painted books! She didn't tell you? Well, I suppose she… I'm not sure… Would you like to see them? Lillian brought them home. There's a lovely copy of *Pride and Prejudice* here…" Cecilia rambled on, leaving the dining room and returning with a basket filled with books that had been beautifully repainted.

He plucked up the copy of *Pride and Prejudice*. It was a clothbound edition, with roses embroidered on the spine. The edges were painted a pale green, with pink hearts dotting the pages, and the center featured a silhouette of two people in Regency attire holding hands.

"It's very nice." He admired her handiwork, marveling at the patience Gianna must have had in order to paint such tiny details on such a small canvas.

His mother had picked up a book and was flipping through its music note–patterned pages.

Crabtree's annual fair was always a topic of much discussion, gossip and anticipation.

This year, the winning entry in the small business category would receive a substantial cash prize for doing the most for the community. Dominic hoped the bookstore would win, though whether it was out of a desire to stay or simply so they could pay for the repairs, he wasn't sure yet.

The doorbell rang, and Dominic instinctively got up to get it, though they were neither in his apartment in Toronto nor his parents' house. Something metallic touched his hand, and he looked down to see his mother pressing a foil-wrapped egg tart on him.

"Sit down and eat, honey," she said as the Chengs hurried to answer the door. "You're looking so pale all of a sudden."

He took a bite, the flaky crust melting in his mouth as he tasted the sweet custard. "Thanks, Mom. It's good."

She beamed, a warm glow of pride suffusing her cheeks.

"Gianna! How good to see you. Lillian is upstairs if you're here to see her," he heard Cecilia say.

His shoulders tensed, his grip tightening on the foil wrapper. Dominic set down the egg tart before he could accidentally crush it. Gianna was here?

He stood when she entered the room. "Good evening, Gianna."

"Oh, I didn't expect to see you, Dominic." Gianna took off her broad-brimmed felt hat, and her hair cascaded around her shoulders in waves. She usually wore her hair in a braid at the store. Why did he notice any changes to her appearance at all? "I just came to drop off something that Lil left at the store."

She handed a bag to Mrs. Cheng. He'd forgotten she was friends with their daughter, Lillian.

Gianna took an egg tart at his mother's invitation and sat next to him. "So, what were you guys talking about? I hope I didn't interrupt."

"We were just looking at the books you said you wanted to enter into the fair." Dominic picked up *Pride and Prejudice* before setting it down again. "I have to say again, I'm impressed by your work."

"Thanks! I hope it wins *some* prize at the fair," she said.

"Well, it had better." He sighed, his shoulders slumping. His mother and the Chengs began their own lively conversation, though he saw his mother glance over from time to time. "Otherwise, I don't know how we'll be paying for these repairs."

Gianna was silent, nibbling on the dessert. She probably resented his pessimism, but someone had to be realistic.

He rubbed a hand over his forehead, doing a mental tally of all the repairs that would need to be done. Dominic had already done it a thousand times on paper, but he wanted to make sure there wasn't some essential item he was forgetting.

"Penny for your thoughts?" Gianna asked.

Without thinking, he blurted out, "I don't know if there's enough money to make the repairs to the store and stay afloat."

"What…what do you mean?" Her half-eaten egg tart fell onto her lap, and she picked it up before dabbing at the resulting grease stain with a napkin.

"What I'm saying is, if we don't get the prize money to pay for these repairs, we'll be dipping into the store's emergency fund, and I don't know if…" He swallowed thickly. "I don't know if we'll be able to keep the lights on, Gianna."

She wiped at her mouth with a tissue. "Can we talk about this outside?"

He set down his egg tart and followed Gianna onto the Chengs' front porch.

Dominic shifted his weight from one foot to the other, trying to remain calm. In reality, his nerves were a raw jumble of live wires.

"Please, don't tell me you're thinking of tearing down the bookstore," Gianna said, her voice soft, like she was treading water around a shark, doing her best not to make a wrong move.

He ran a hand through his hair. "Gianna, I don't know. I'm considering my options, and gutting the place is still one of those choices. After what happened—"

"Don't you think the bookstore can be saved?" Her voice rose, and she took a step closer to him. The tips of her sneakers brushed against his loafers, and the air seemed charged with an energy he couldn't describe. "Don't you think there's any hope for it?"

He heard the wind rustle through the pines, and the faint scent of pine needles reached him. The night was so still, without even the sound of a passing car, that all he could focus on was her. "You're an idealist, Gianna."

"I know I'm doing what your grandfather would have wanted me to do." Her brown eyes were determined as they glared up at him. She folded her arms over her chest.

"You—" Dominic took a deep breath, trying and failing to steady himself. "You know nothing about what my grandfather would have wanted."

"I know he left the store to you," she said. "Do you think he did that because he wanted his grandson to just tear it down? Or because he thought you would take good care of it?"

"Gianna, I have a son to worry about."

"The bookstore is your responsibility, too."

Dominic sighed. "This bookstore is more than I anticipated. It's not as simple as merely keeping the store afloat. The amount of repairs that would have to be done is substantial. I mean, the air conditioning, the ceiling, the pipe… It's a lot, Gianna."

"I know you think I'm just an immature child who doesn't understand how a business is run. But let me remind you that I've been the manager at this place for two years, and I've been working at Tang's for five years, Dominic. I'm not going to let you just *give up* on the bookstore so easily."

Give up.

The words rang in his ears. Was that what he was doing? Giving up on his responsibilities and running away from his duties? He'd thought that turning the bookstore into an office space would be the sensible thing to do. But now he was beginning to wonder if reason and responsibility weren't always compatible. He was beginning to wonder if following his heart and his responsibilities might be one and the same—that he might have to take a risk in order to fulfill this duty.

Gianna's tone softened. "It's only been two weeks. Please, at least give it another week, Dominic."

He clenched his jaw. He didn't want to be swayed by her softer tone and pleading eyes. He *definitely* didn't want to be swayed by the look she was giving him that spoke of vulnerability and desperation. What bothered him the most was the fact that Gianna Marchesi was the most stubborn woman he had ever met. And that he was about to agree with her.

"Fine. I'll stay." He was many things, but he wasn't a quitter. "But we'd better pray we win the prize for the best small business at the fair, because the money would go a long way toward funding the renovations that need to be done."

She gave him a surprisingly fierce glare for a woman who was a good head shorter than him. "Yes, well, I guess this whole thing is just about money to you."

He raked a hand through his hair. Of course it was about money! He had no job right now and a son to support. How could it not be about money? He tried a bit of levity. "I've heard it's what makes the world go round."

"That's *love*." Her glower barely dimmed in intensity. "And if you don't know that, maybe you don't belong at Tang's, anyway."

Dominic shouldn't have felt as lonely as he did when Gianna walked back into the house, the screen door slamming behind her. But his heart ached with remorse, and he rubbed his hands over his arms as an unseasonably chilly summer breeze gusted across the porch.

How were the two of them going to get along, let alone run a bookstore together?

Chapter Eight

Whatever semblance of a good working relationship he and Gianna might have created had evaporated in one day, and Dominic only had himself to blame.

The air was filled with more tension than usual. Garrett even cast a sidelong glance between Dominic and Gianna as though asking what had gone wrong. Dominic merely shrugged, though he knew all too well he'd made a mistake.

He never had a chance to talk to Gianna about their argument the previous night, because the bookstore had so many customers that he might have thought God had arranged it that way to keep them from speaking. Perhaps it was God's grace since Dominic might have said another foolish thing if they'd spoken that day. It also allowed him to see that instead of the lifeless monotony he'd expected, the bookstore was thriving. Of course, based on the accounts he'd been combing through in the back office, he knew that was true, but it was nice to see proof of it in real life.

Customers lingered in the bookstore with coffees, teenagers huddled in groups on the beanbag chairs and several people pushed strollers as they walked through the shelves, rooting through the stacks for the perfect book. Even with the damage done to the store, business had picked up again after they reopened, and most of the store's problem areas could be hidden. The sales were better than he'd expected, as well. Perhaps the bookstore might make more profit from remaining as it was, after all.

Yet none of it would go smoothly if he and Gianna didn't get along.

Dominic had spent approximately seventeen hours and forty-six minutes (not that he was counting) existing in this awkward limbo with Gianna, while he wondered whether his response to her had been a mistake. No, not wondered. He *knew* it had been, but he didn't know what to do about it.

Finally, Emmett asked him about their

change in behavior after dinner, when they had been both assigned dish duty. "Dad, how come Gianna is mad at you?"

"What makes you think she's mad at me?" he said, not about to deny it.

"She keeps asking me to pass on messages to you instead of talking to you herself. That's what Grandma does when she's mad at Grandpa. And then, under her breath, I heard her call you a *mer-sin-ary*. Is that a kind of bird? Like a canary?"

"That's a grown-up word, just like this is a grown-up problem that you don't need to worry about, okay, buddy?" He rinsed off a bowl and passed it to Emmett, who placed it in the dishwasher.

"Is this about the store?" Emmett asked. "Because I…you know, knocked over all those shelves?"

"This has *nothing* to do with you, Emmett," he said firmly.

Perhaps *too* firmly. Because Emmett dropped the fork he had been holding into the dishwasher and crossed his arms over his chest. "I don't want to talk to you. You're being a…a big jerk!"

"Buddy, you know I didn't mean it like that," he said, following Emmett as he stomped toward the refrigerator. "I just meant that this fight isn't about you, okay?"

Emmett's ensuing silence was sullen.

His son opened the fridge, staring at the string cheese on the top shelf that he could not reach. Then he slammed it shut and marched toward the living room.

"Don't treat your grandparents' property that way," he said, planting a hand on the counter to keep his son from getting away. He ducked under his arm, trying to escape their conversation. Dominic gripped his son under the armpits and began tickling him.

"Let me go, Dad!" Emmett yelled, squirming out of his father's hold.

"Apologize," he said. "And stop slamming doors. One of these days, you're going to break something that can't be fixed."

"No!" Emmett aimed a kick at his knee, and Dominic decided his son had gotten his stubborn streak from him. "I'm not sorry!"

He lifted up his son so that their faces were level and looked him in the eye. "Emmett, I know you don't mean that."

To his surprise, his son stopped fighting, his body going limp as he averted his gaze from Dominic's. After a few moments, he let out what sounded like a sob.

Immediately, Dominic rearranged his grasp and pulled his son into his chest. "What's wrong? Did I hurt you?"

When Emmett finally spoke, his voice was strained, and Dominic's shirt was wet with tears. "I like Gianna… She's nice to me… And I like being in Crabtree, and I love living with Grandma and Grandpa… I don't want you and Gianna to fight because then we'll have to go back to Toronto, and I don't like it there anymore."

Something cracked in his heart, leaving him raw. Exposed. He took a deep breath before he spoke. "What's wrong with Toronto? I thought you liked living there. You have friends at school…and your karate classes are there."

Emmett shook his head, his dark curls bouncing with the movement. "All my friends are moving to a different school. And the other kids at the karate dojo always make fun of me. And when we're in Toronto, you're always working and you never have time for me. Plus, Grandma always makes good food like dim sum and stuff."

He tried to process his son's words without wanting to take care of every bully his son had mentioned. Yes, he worked long hours, but his father had done the same, and Dominic had turned out all right. Hadn't he? Surely, his son knew that he loved him even if he couldn't spend all his time with him. Didn't providing for him financially mean something?

But now, looking down at his son's tearful face, he realized that all the hours he had put in at the accounting firm didn't mean anything.

"You can go to a different karate dojo and you'll see your friends outside of school. I can cut back my hours, too, and we can have dim sum in Chinatown."

"The Chinese food in Toronto doesn't taste the same as how Grandma makes it."

Dominic sighed. He opened the fridge and pulled out a string cheese. "You've given me a lot to think about. Let's talk about this later, kiddo."

"Thanks, Dad." Emmett took the snack but hesitated before unwrapping it. "Can you ask Gianna to show me how to make baked risotto? If we have to leave Crabtree, I want to eat it again in Toronto."

He ruffled his son's hair, glad he was in good enough of a mood to think about food. "Sure thing, bud."

* * *

Gianna had just locked up Tang's after her shift on Friday, Dominic and Emmett having left an hour earlier for reasons she couldn't remember, when she found an all-too-familiar man standing in front of her car, holding a bouquet of pink peonies, with a young boy at his side. "I… I thought you had gone home for the day. What are you doing here? Why do you have flowers?"

Dominic took a step toward her. Behind him, Emmett shoved his hands into his pockets and stared down at his scuffed sneakers. "I'm here, with flowers, because I wanted—no, *needed*—to apologize to you." Then, as if registering that his son was still standing there, Dominic added, "Want to wait in the car, buddy?"

The young boy nodded. "Can I have your keys? I want to listen to the radio."

"I'll unlock the car for you, but no playing with the windows," he said.

Despite her shock, Gianna smiled, watching their little negotiation. It reminded her of Luca and her father when Luca had been Emmett's age. Only… Dominic was nothing like Luca or her father. He had a certain quiet presence, a certain subtle confidence, one that

didn't demand to be seen or heard but was noticed and remembered all the same. If only
he didn't have a clinical professional outlook
that valued efficiency and money above all
else… And if only he didn't look so adorably
charming while holding a bouquet of her favorite flowers.

"I'm sure you didn't come here to risk your
son's life in a vehicle accident, so get on with
the apology." She waved a hand.

His throat bobbed as he swallowed. "Gianna, the things I said to you the other night
were, well… Yes, I'm worried about the store
because of the whole money issue. But it's not
just about money."

"I'm listening." She tilted her head to one
side.

He sighed. "It's important for the bookstore to be thriving. I'm sure you know that.
But… I have a son. And sometimes it feels
like, ever since he was born, all I've been
doing is solving one problem or another. It's
like Whac-A-Mole. The second I think one
thing is solved, another issue pops up. I've
been spending this whole week wondering if
I'm a horrible father for letting Emmett mess
up the store, then wondering if I'm doing the
wrong thing by gutting the bookstore, or if I'd

be doing the right thing to just cut my losses and sell the place..."

Dominic fiddled with the top button of his flannel shirt. He looked like he was wondering if he should have told her so much, but whatever regrets he might have about telling her all this, she wanted to silence them. She wanted to soothe his worries, to tell him that the bookstore was a fantastic investment, but if she was being honest, even she had had doubts crack through her usually optimistic mindset.

"Go on." She rocked back and forth on her heels. Gianna felt bad for having misjudged him as a heartless businessman. He was a concerned father beneath his gruff exterior, and he *was* in financial distress, after all.

"What I'm trying to say is, all I want is for my son to have a stable future. The last thing I want is for his life to be any more unpredictable than it has been. I'm sure you can understand that."

Her tense posture uncoiled, and a smile appeared on her lips. "I think I see where you're coming from."

He cracked a smile. "I hope you can forgive me."

"Well," she said, sniffing the peonies again,

"the flowers certainly helped. How did you know these are my favorites?"

He shrugged. "You always have them in the store."

Beep! A horn honked, startling her out of her skin. Her knees went to jelly, and she nearly dropped the flowers, staring at the source of the sound.

"Emmett!" Dominic called, looking over at his silver sedan, which was parked a few feet away.

"Sorry, Dad!"

Gianna giggled. "What are you two doing now? Do you want to grab dinner or something?"

"Actually…" He turned toward the car again. "Emmett, come here and tell Gianna what your evening plans are."

Moments later, the seven-year-old boy hopped out of the car and skipped toward them, avoiding each crack in the pavement as he did so. "Gianna, can you *please* teach me how to make baked risotto?"

Her shoulders slumped at his request, her heart heavy in her chest. "I don't think so, buddy."

"But why? Don't you know how?" Emmett's brown eyes were wide and pleading as he gazed up at her. He held his hands behind his back, rocking forward and back on his heels. "Is it because I knocked over the shelves? I'll pay for it with my college fund—"

"No, no," she blurted out. "It's not that at all, Emmett. I just… I just don't make it as good as my dad does, that's all."

That was only half the truth, but Emmett nodded, looking both satisfied and thoughtful. "That's okay, my dad is a good cook. He can just get the recipe from your dad, and then he'll make it for me."

She looked at Dominic for confirmation. "Is that true?"

"Don't sound so surprised. I've been a bachelor for almost a decade—I had to learn how to cook or Emmett and I would've starved by now." Dominic grinned at her, and she could see something of the twenty-year-old he was when the responsibility of a man had been thrust upon him. "Do you want to come to my parents' house for dinner?"

She considered it, then decided that there couldn't be any harm in agreeing. "Sure."

Chapter Nine

When they got to his parents' house, Dominic found a note on the foyer table telling him that his parents had gone out to dinner and would be home around eight. So he got to work in the kitchen while Emmett ran upstairs to clean up.

Dominic considered his options. There was the potential for a great deal of embarrassment if he made Italian food in front of a woman whose parents ran an Italian-Chinese restaurant. Nor was Chinese food his forte, since he'd left home so long ago that his mother had never been able to fulfill her vow to teach him to cook. Though he *said* he knew how to cook, his skills were limited to easy, cheap meals like quesadillas, ramen and salads. He'd once tried to roast a whole chicken, but it had not worked out so well. Realizing that this was more of an apology dinner than a three-course Michelin-star meal, he decided on tacos.

"Do you want me to help?" Gianna asked. She sat with a relaxed smile on one of the bar stools, looking far too at home in the space. She looked more at ease in Crabtree than he had ever felt. Gianna Marchesi *belonged* here, a staple of the town like Marchesi's or Tang's. "I don't want to just sit around and do nothing."

"You're a guest. My mother would have my head for not offering you something to drink." He pulled out defrosted chicken thighs and ground beef from the bottom shelf of the fridge.

"I'd ask for coffee, but I'm afraid you'll tell me it's too late in the day for a cup."

"I can't judge you for the same habits I have." Dominic washed his hands, then went about brewing a pot of coffee. "How do you take it?"

"Black, please," she said.

"A woman after my own heart," he joked. It was easier to interact with her here. Though he owned the bookstore, it felt more like her territory. His parents' house was neutral ground.

He flavored the meats with a hefty dose of taco seasoning that he found in his parents' fridge, then chopped the chicken into cubes while Gianna hovered around the coffeepot like she wanted to pour it directly into her mouth. He chuckled at the thought.

"What's so funny?" Her tone wasn't defensive, merely curious, with a hint of surprise as she planted a hand on her hip, looking over at him. The posture emphasized the cut of her dress, a summery frock in a shade of mustard that looked particularly beautiful on her.

"You're inches away from the coffeepot like it's your source of life," he said.

"I'll admit to having one of those wooden signs in my home that says All I Need Is a Little Bit of Coffee and a Whole Lot of Jesus," she said sheepishly. "Oh, hi, Emmett!"

His son skidded across the hardwood floor in socks, nearly running directly into Gianna. She caught him easily enough, holding him at arms' length with her hands on his shoulders. His hair was damp, a few curls plastered to his forehead.

"Whoa there, buddy," Dominic said. "What did I say about running indoors and breaking things by accident?"

When he'd mentioned it before, Emmett

had looked resigned and yielded to Dominic's scolding. Today, he looked mischievous, which was either very good or supremely bad. He stepped back so that Gianna's hands fell off of his arms. "You said not to do anything that could break things indoors. I didn't break anything, and I wasn't running—I was *sliding*."

Rolling his eyes, Dominic tousled his son's wet hair. "You're too smart for your own good. Do you want to help me? We're making tacos. You can grate the cheese."

Emmett's eyes lit up. He loved all dairy products, for reasons unbeknown to Dominic, who had grown up lactose intolerant and to this day still had nightmares about ice cream.

"What kind of cheese do you guys have?" Gianna asked, pouring two cups of coffee and passing one to Dominic.

"Thank you," he said, sipping it. It warmed him in places he hadn't realized he was cold, even though it was seventy-five degrees outside. Or maybe that was her smile and the brush of her fingers against his.

"All of them," Emmett said cheerfully. "Gouda, Brie, string cheese… But my favorite is marble cheddar."

"Good choice," Gianna said with a nod. "Clearly a young man of exquisite taste."

Emmett beamed at her. "What does *exquisite* mean?"

Gianna defined the word for him, correcting his pronunciation. As Gianna and Emmett launched into a conversation about cheese, with Gianna telling him about buffalo cheese made only in a special region of Italy, Dominic got to work dicing the vegetables into fine pieces, then putting them all into different bowls. The last steps were to cook the meats, then warm the taco shells (hard shells for Emmett, since he liked his shells to shatter into nacho chips) and grab the sour cream and salsa from the fridge.

Just as he tossed the chicken and beef in the frying pans and turned on the stove, he heard a cry of pain. "Ow!"

Dominic looked up with alarm and crossed the kitchen in three strides. Was Emmett hurt? Gianna?

"He just cut his finger on the cheese grater. Don't worry, I've done it dozens of times, so I'm an old pro at taking care of these kinds of injuries." Gianna turned back toward Emmett. "Does it hurt?"

Emmett shook his head bravely, his quivering lower lip belying the tough image he wanted to project. "N-no."

Dominic looked at his son's finger, which was bleeding. "Let's get you cleaned up."

Gianna cleared her throat. "Is something burning?"

"Oh, no," he muttered, not wanting to race back toward the pan even as the acrid smell of smoke reached his nostrils. "Can you take care of him?"

"Of course," she said, ushering Emmett toward the bathroom before looking over her shoulder to ask, "Where do your parents keep the first aid kit?"

"In the bathroom medicine cabinet," he called back, fixing all his attention on keeping the food from burning.

It felt startlingly easy to trust Gianna Marchesi with his son.

Too easy.

Chapter Ten

"I can do it myself," Emmett protested as Gianna rinsed his finger under the sink, patted it dry with gauze and wrapped it with a Spider-Man Band-Aid.

"I know," she said calmly. It was the same reaction that Luca had had when he was around Emmett's age and had cut *his* finger while making mac and cheese after their father had banned boxed versions from the house as an "abomination."

"Do you think my dad likes you?" Emmett asked when she had finished bandaging his finger. He didn't hop off the counter, just dangled his Spider-Man-sock-clad feet off the edge.

Gianna dropped the box of superhero-themed Band-Aids she'd been holding. "We get along well enough."

"No, I meant as in *like like*," Emmett clarified.

"And what would you know about that, mister? You're too young to *like like* anybody, and I'm sure your father would agree with that," she said, picking up the Band-Aids and putting them in the medicine cabinet. She turned to face him.

"My friend said that in middle school, guys get flowers for the girls they *like like*." Emmett eyed her with curiosity like she was a frog he was dissecting in science class. "Is that true?"

"Sometimes," she said.

"I like your hair," Emmett said abruptly.

Gianna relaxed, chuckling to herself. "Thanks, kiddo. I like your hair, too."

Emmett nodded, one curl flopping over his forehead and covering his eye. The kid needed a haircut soon. "It's wavy like mine. My dad and my grandpa and my grandma doesn't have hair like me."

"*Don't* have hair like you," she corrected.

"They don't." He nodded, still swinging his legs. "But our hair looks the same."

She glanced in the mirror. If she were a bit older, or Emmett younger, strangers might very well think they were related. They were both half Chinese, half white, though her Italian heritage lent her a more olive complexion, and his eyes were a different shape.

She wondered what it would be like if Dominic did *like like* her and Emmett were her son.

Gianna cleared her throat. "I think I smell something delicious. Why don't we go see if the food's ready?"

Emmett carefully got off the counter, one foot at a time, rather than hopping off. She nearly laughed but didn't want to draw attention to the cautious movement.

"Dinner's ready!" Dominic called.

"Perfect timing," Gianna said. "Race you to the table?"

"Dad said no running in the house," Emmett said. "Right, Dad?"

Dominic rubbed the nape of his neck with a mismatched floral oven mitt: one was red with roses, the other pink with carnations. Paired with his flannel shirt and khakis, the effect was rather humorous. "That's right."

They walked toward the table at a sedate speed instead, Emmett putting a little spring in his step as he spotted the food. He threw himself into the chair to the left of Dominic, who sat at the head. Unsure of where to seat herself, Gianna took the seat on Dominic's right. She realized with a little surprise that if they had been a family, they might have sat like this, the three of them around the long dining table. Gianna shook her head, putting the thought out of her mind, and smoothed out her yellow dress. She was reading too much into a simple dinner.

"Let's say grace," Dominic suggested, reaching first for Emmett's hand, then, more tentatively, for Gianna's, a silent question in his eyes.

She placed her hand in his, trying to ignore the faint calluses on his palm—didn't he work a desk job? How did he have calluses?—and the way his fingers engulfed her smaller ones. The grip made her feel…safe. And when Emmett reached his hand across the table, straining to reach her hand, she took it, and she almost felt like the image she had had of the three of them as a family was complete.

"Heavenly Father, thank You for bringing Gianna to eat dinner with us today," Dominic began. "We would like to thank You for the food You have provided to us. May it nourish us and may You bless the conversations we have. In Jesus's name, we pray. Amen."

They let go of each other's hands, Gianna

feeling oddly bereft even as she picked up a hard taco shell.

"You like hard shells, too?" Emmett piped up, watching her as she ate. She was amused by the close attention he paid to her, but also slightly worried. As Gianna scooped ground beef and beans into her taco shell, she wondered how it would feel if Dominic decided to leave Crabtree and return to the big city, uprooting not only her life but his son's. She would miss him and Emmett; she was sure of it now.

"Um, yeah. They're the best," she said, trying to hide her concern as she took a bite of her now overflowing taco. "Yum. My compliments to the chef."

"I'm glad you approve, even if you chose the *inferior* taco shells," he said, having selected a soft tortilla that he was eating with significantly less mess.

She shrugged. "I like the crunch. And, life is messy. Tacos should reflect life."

Dominic laughed. He was more relaxed this evening than she'd seen him in the past few weeks. "So your opinion on taco shells is based on…a culinary philosophy of life?"

"Isn't everything in life an analogy for food?" Gianna's tone turned thoughtful.

* * *

"Everything in life is an analogy for food when your family runs a restaurant."

Part of Dominic wanted to test her reaction at the mention of Marchesi's. Earlier, when Emmett had asked her to teach him how to make the baked risotto, he suspected there was more to her refusal than a simple belief in her inadequate cooking skills. No, Dominic thought there might be something more to it than that. And he was determined to find out.

He wanted to peel back the layers of her cheerful personality and the tenacious spirit that made her fight for the bookstore she loved. Dominic wanted to see who Gianna Marchesi was because…he had the suspicion that *she* already knew who *he* was. Perhaps, just by observing him, Gianna might know him better than he thought.

"I guess my family's business has influenced me that way," she said. "Everything's a metaphor for food."

"Your *family's* business, not yours?" he asked, biting into his taco.

"I know everyone in town has always seen me as just another one of the Marchesis. Plus, there's my middle-child syndrome, always being overlooked," she said. "I guess

I just wanted to branch out from the restaurant and…be independent. Start something of my own."

"But you didn't want to start your own business?" he probed.

She shrugged. "Tang's has always been an oasis for me. I love books, and it grew into a love of art, too, when I saw the beautiful books your granddad had in the store. Plus, my house has always been a bit crazy and loud with two siblings and my cousins coming over, so the store was a quiet place I'd always sneak off to, for reading and doing homework."

"I remember seeing you there," he confessed. Once or twice, when he'd gone by after school to help Grandpa with the bookstore, he'd seen the same brunette curled up on the beanbag chair, nose stuck in a book or bent over the small table in the corner, studying. He'd recognized her as Luca's sister, though they'd never really spoken. "Grandpa would ask me to work with him in the store when I was in middle school. Then when high school rolled around, I got caught up with other activities and stopped going."

His grandfather and the bookstore had drifted off his list of priorities, though he'd still seen his grandpa every week or so for family dinners. That was, until he'd left with Emmett.

"Do you wish you had stayed?" Gianna asked. "I mean, kept working at the store?"

He shrugged. "It wasn't really like working for me, more like volunteering with the promise of a free milkshake from the Crabtree Diner afterward. But... I don't know. I guess things might be different if I had."

Who knows? He might have met Gianna earlier, and she might have been more to him than Luca's little sister. They might have—

"Yeah," she said. "It's funny how everything in life can change just from one simple decision."

He finished his taco and reached for another tortilla, suddenly realizing it was the last one. "Do you want it?"

"No, I'm stuffed. You go ahead. I'll wash up," she said, getting up and taking her and Emmett's plates. Emmett had excused himself from dinner and their conversation a while ago, and Dominic could hear the music and sound effects of *Mario Kart* from the living room.

"You're a guest. I can't let you wash up," he said, getting up to take the plates from *her*.

"But you cooked, so it's only fair that I clean," she protested, trying to take the plates from *him*.

They were inches apart. He realized that at this angle, with her fingers sliding against his, her head tilted back to look up at him, the fire in her brown eyes burning so bright, he could have kissed her.

And that he might want to.

Keys jingled in the lock at the back door, and both of them jumped away from each other. Plates in her hands, Gianna raised them in victory. "I guess I'll do the dishes?"

Dominic took a deep breath. "Sure. I guess you win this round."

"Dom, honey, how was dinner?" his mother asked as she exited the foyer, entering the dining room. "I hope you and Emmett didn't miss us too much."

"Where's my favorite grandson?" his father said, pretending to scour the room for Emmett before he heard the sounds of the Wii console. "Ah, time for me to beat him at *Mario Kart*."

His mother scanned the dining room. "This looks like a lot of food for just two people."

Just then, Gianna came out of the kitchen wearing rubber gloves. Her hair was tied back into a messy bun, exposing the slope of her neck and the cross necklace at her collarbone. "Dominic, where do your parents keep the dish soap—oh, hi, Mrs. Tang. It's so good to see you again!"

"Gianna, lovely to see you, too. But why is my son making you do the dishes? You're a guest here," his mother said, marching across the room and shooting him a why-didn't-you-stop-her? look.

He didn't tell her that he'd already tried. "Did you guys have dessert yet?"

Summoned by the word *dessert*, Emmett slid into the kitchen in his socks again. "There's dessert?"

"Yes, of course, there is," his mother said absentmindedly, her gaze sliding back to Gianna. Then to Dominic. Then it darted between the two of them, and he suspected there were far too many thoughts churning in his mother's mind.

"Great, then let's have dessert," Gianna said, taking off the gloves and hurrying to escape his mother's scrutiny.

However, it was impossible to evade *that*.

First, Dominic made the mistake of holding out a chair for Gianna, causing Dominic's mother to eye her like a future daughter-in-law. Then, over black sesame pudding with *tong yun*, Emmett made the second crucial error of asking Gianna if she wanted to play basketball with him, Luca, Dominic and Pietro sometime. This had the immediate effect of causing his father to sit up, look up from his pudding and view her as a potential candidate for Dominic's bride.

Throughout the brief exchange, Dominic's mother managed to pepper her with a never-ending succession of questions as though this were an interview. Did she know how to cook Chinese food? (Yes, she and Estella had spent their childhoods toddling after their mother, which included following her around the kitchen and to Crabtree's lone Asian supermarket.) Could she speak Chinese at all? (Rudimentary Cantonese.) Did she want to have children in the future? (To this, Gianna stammered that she loved children but had yet to find any man to have them with.)

Perturbed by his mother's interrogation, Dominic cleared his throat. "Mom, I think that's an intrusive question—"

"What? I'm just making conversation," she protested.

Emmett was seated next to Gianna and asked her to teach him how to make funny shapes with his cloth napkin, ending the discussion of that subject, for which she appeared grateful. She started folding hers into an animal.

This only led Dominic's mother to turn her attention to Dominic, however, and bring up his high-school accomplishments.

"You know, Dominic was a Mathlete in high school. He even won a trophy," his mother informed Gianna as she showed Emmett how to form his napkin into the shape of an elephant.

"Oh, really?" Gianna perked up. "Did you have a Mathletes uniform? Are there pictures?"

"Mom…" he groaned.

"Of course, how careless of me to mention it and then not bring out the family photo album. I'll go get it right now." With that, she got up from her seat and walked—no, sprinted—toward the living room, where they kept their photo albums.

Gianna reached across the table and patted him on the forearm. "I like your mom. She's funny."

"She can be a lot." He turned his hand over so that their palms touched, almost absentmindedly. He felt not only warm but alive at the brush of her fingers against his. Emmett didn't seem to notice, engrossed in his napkin folding.

"All of us are in some way," she said. "It's what makes life interesting."

"Look, I made an elephant!" Emmett said, showing them his folded napkin.

Gianna high-fived him, then Emmett yawned. Dominic felt the loss of her hand far too keenly.

He stood. "All right, I think it's time for you to go to bed, buddy. It's past nine, and that means it's way past your bedtime."

"But I don't wanna," Emmett said, yawning again. "Do I have to?"

"Yes," he said, as sternly as he could. "You have to. So say good-night to your grandparents and Gianna—"

"Can Gianna read me a story before I go to bed?" Emmett asked.

"I thought you said you wanted *me* to read to you," Dominic said.

Emmett tapped on his chin, looking thoughtful for a seven-year-old boy. "You can both read to me. You can do the boy voices, and Gianna can do the girl voices. Right?"

"I don't mind, Dominic, but if you don't feel comfortable with it…" Gianna said, putting down her spoon and a half-eaten bowl of pudding.

He considered the matter. How did he feel, once he got past the initial surprise of his son's request? It wasn't that he felt betrayed by Emmett choosing someone else over him—no, his son had asked for his grandma or grandpa to read him a story or play video games with him before—but he was worried. Was Emmett getting too attached to Gianna?

"Oh, it's not a big deal. Just read him the story," his father suggested. "Your mother and I would like some alone time, anyway."

"Oh, I didn't mean to intrude—" Gianna began.

"Nonsense," his father said. "Go on and get Emmett to bed."

Dominic let Emmett and Gianna go ahead of him up the stairs as Emmett led her by the hand toward his room, which had been Dominic's childhood bedroom. "I have a race-car bed! And cool Spider-Man posters. And a sword."

"Whoa, a sword?" Gianna said with a grin. "Do you use it to slice off the heads of monsters?"

"No, it's a practice sword for tai chi, and my grandpa gave it to me," Emmett said, chattering on happily. "Look, I can do cool moves with it and stuff—"

"It's a little too late for that, Emmett," he said. "Why don't you show her your sword-fighting moves another time?"

Emmett yawned. "Okay, Dad. I'm gonna change into my pj's real quick."

"Don't forget to brush your teeth and floss," Dominic said as Emmett grabbed his pajamas and ran into the bathroom.

"I never forget!" he called back, which made Dominic chuckle. Emmett had had more than one cavity before, so he doubted that.

Gianna gazed around the small bedroom, arms folded over her chest, looking like she was absorbing every detail of the space.

"Thanks for agreeing to do this," he said, clearing his throat. "You didn't have to."

"I lo—I like Emmett," she said, correcting herself. "He's a great kid. I apologize if I was overstepping my boundaries, though…"

"Gianna—" He paused. "You've been terrific with Emmett, and I don't mind you being here. I guess I've been alone for so long, I've never let anyone take care of Emmett, except a babysitter or my parents."

"That's understandable. I don't want to push your boundaries, Dominic. If you don't want me to be here..." Gianna looked up at him, a lock of hair falling over her face, shielding her brown eyes from view.

He tucked the strands behind her ear without thinking. "I do enjoy having you here when we're not...ah, getting into unnecessary arguments."

"Mostly on your part, but I agree with that statement," she said, stepping closer to him. There was an expectant look in her eyes. He tucked his hands in his pockets, unsure of what to say.

"Dad? Gianna?" The door cracked open, and Emmett stuck his head inside. "I'm ready for bed now."

Taking a deep breath, Gianna smoothed out her dress. Why was she so nervous? She had babysat plenty of children, watched her younger cousins countless times before and had also helped out in the church nursery for a while. There was no reason for her to be anxious about reading a bedtime story to Emmett Tang.

Though maybe that wasn't what was causing her palms to sweat and her heart to beat wildly. It was more likely the presence of his father leading to those anxious symptoms.

"What do you want to read, Emmett?" Dominic asked, crouching down next to Emmett's race car–shaped bed.

Emmett was clad in Spider-Man pajamas, and the blue-and-red pattern matched the sheets he was under. The bedroom walls were lined with slightly dusty shelves, one holding a basketball trophy. She squinted to read the name in the dim lighting of the room. It gleamed to show the words *Dominic Tang*. She guessed that this had been his bedroom before he'd left for Toronto.

"I want Gianna to pick," he suggested, pointing at one of the full bookshelves. There was a pile of comics next to a heap of books. Emmett was a precocious child and clearly bright for his age.

It was sweet that he was willing to have his father read to him. At his age, Luca had been willful, choosing to play with various pieces of sports equipment even at bedtime rather than be read to. Once, he'd swung a baseball bat while jumping on his bed and hit the ceiling fan.

"How about this?" She chose a book she knew was currently popular with boys Emmett's age.

Emmett grinned at her, a gap-toothed smile

that shone more brightly than the orange lamp. "I love that one."

"Great." She felt relieved at making an appropriate choice, as if this were a test. It must have been Dominic's gaze on her, making her feel under scrutiny, off-balance, even when he looked awkward on the too-small chair beside Emmett's bed.

Gianna lowered herself onto the beanbag chair next to Dominic and opened the book to where an orange bookmark stuck out. "You can go first."

He took the book and began reading, though he first gave Emmett a sheepish look. "One chapter. And, I'm not sure there are any 'girl voices.'"

"That's fine. I did the most important part." She shifted on her beanbag chair, resisting the urge to lean her head against Dominic's shoulder. "You read it. You have a nice voice."

A blush rose in her cheeks. Why had she said that? It was true, his voice was soothing and deep, but she hadn't needed to tell him.

"Dad," Emmett urged. "Hurry up and read it."

Dominic cleared his throat and read the chapter. Gianna let herself be carried away by the familiar story. Emmett's yawning protests that he wasn't tired, Dominic's voice tugging her into the story world and the soft murmur of the wind rustling through the cracked-open window all lulled her into a comforting thought: that she might be a family with Emmett and Dominic someday.

"That's it?" Emmett said in alarm, jolting Gianna out of her thoughts. "That's the end of the chapter? Please, Dad, one more…"

"No, it's late," Dominic said firmly. "We can continue the story tomorrow night."

"Fine," Emmett said with a huff.

"Good night, buddy." Dominic stood up from the chair and bent down to kiss Emmett on the forehead. "Sweet dreams."

She echoed the words, squeezing Emmett's small hand. "Night."

"Night, Gianna. Night, Dad."

"Don't forget to say your prayers," said Dominic.

Emmett scrambled out of bed, kneeling beside his nightstand.

Dominic held open the bedroom door for Gianna to walk through and left it ajar behind them. For a moment, they stood silently in the hallway, listening to Emmett pray.

"Dear Jesus, I know I've been praying the same thing for a long time, and maybe You're sick of it by now, but my dad said that those who pray without stopping will have their prayers answered. So God, I'm praying that You would bring me a brother. Or even a sister. I don't care as long as we can play together. Please, God? Amen."

Dominic had turned white. He closed the door with a soft click, looking like he wished he had never heard Emmett's prayer.

Gianna didn't know what to do. Should she comfort him? Just pretend she hadn't heard it and leave?

Finally, Dominic cleared his throat. "I'm sorry you had to hear that… This was a mistake…"

"A mistake?" She had the sudden feeling that he meant more than them listening at Emmett's door. Gianna was scared that he meant the entire night. The flowers, the dinner, the story. Everything she'd thought might be glimpses of something more—they'd all been nothing more than a mistake to him. A lapse in judgment.

"I'm sorry," he said again.

"Don't be." She swallowed, her throat tight. "Don't be sorry, Dominic. I care about Emmett, and it's natural for kids to want to have siblings. There's nothing for you to regret or be embarrassed over."

Dominic shook his head. "All these years, I thought I was doing my best as a father. But now I see that even that isn't enough because I've failed at one of the most fundamental things my son needs—"

"Dominic, no, that can't be true. When I was growing up, there were so many times I thought I'd rather be an only child than have siblings."

"But you love your siblings, don't you?" he challenged her, his brown eyes boring into hers with an intensity she couldn't quite place.

"Yeah," she said, shoulders slumping. "I do."

"I always wanted siblings, too," he said with a shrug. "But my parents had me too late in life to consider it."

"That's not the case for you," she breathed.

"No, but…my son's mother abandoned him. Emmett and I are —" Dominic cut himself off. "What woman would want to saddle herself with a man with a rowdy seven-year-old from another woman?"

"That can't be true," she said. "I'm sure that if you…"

"I don't want to take away time I should

be spending with my son to waste it on a woman who might decide she doesn't even want him." He shook his head. "Emmett is my priority. Not anyone else."

His sorrowful, heavy, *pained* words buried a sliver of ice deep in her heart. "I'm sorry you feel that way."

Dominic sighed. "Thanks for having dinner with us tonight."

"Of course." The way he said *us* told her he saw himself and Emmett as a two-person unit, unable to ever let anyone else in no matter how much either of them might want to. Both of them too scared to make their needs known or even try to fulfill them.

"Good night, Dominic." Surprising even herself, she reached up on tiptoe and pressed a kiss to his cheek, feeling the stubble on his jaw.

Then she marched down the hall, her heart beating double time, as she left him standing alone.

Chapter Eleven

Dominic had never been a fan of arts and crafts growing up. Having a son who preferred sports to staying inside and whose favorite indoor activity was reading didn't help him in that department, either. But now he was changing his mind about his artistic skills as he, Gianna and Emmett huddled themselves over the books that needed to be painted in the back of the bookstore. They sat at a table with an assortment of paintbrushes, books and palettes that lay on top of some newspaper for easier cleanup.

Emmett was fiddling with the brim of his Toronto Raptors cap while waving his paintbrush around.

"You're going to get paint on your nose, Emmett," Gianna chided him with a smile as she approached him with a wet paper towel. "Here. At least clean off your brush first."

"Okay, G," Emmett said, taking the towel from her and wiping the brush with it.

Dominic chuckled. "Impressive. He never listens when I tell him to put his plate in the sink."

"You just need to use the right tone." Gianna winked at him before returning to work on the book in front of her.

Emmett was practicing on one of the damaged books. He listened intently as Gianna described the painstaking process of painting a book. It wasn't as simple as Dominic had thought.

First, they wrapped both covers of the hardback in white paper to keep paint from getting onto the original covers. After that, special clamps were required to hold the pages together and create as flat of a painting surface as possible. Then, the painting began. He watched her do it first: spraying the edge with a base coat, then waiting for it to dry before adding more decoration.

He didn't know why, but he enjoyed watching her work—the way her nose scrunched when she was working on a minute detail, or the way she gave a small, satisfied smile when something turned out just right. Though he still wouldn't call himself a painter, he found himself enjoying the process and the aftermath.

"What are you looking at?" Gianna glanced up from the book she was painting—*Wuthering Heights*—and fixed her gaze on him.

He hesitated, then said, "You."

"I can't see how that could be at all interesting." A coy smile played on her lips, but it was tempered by something else in her eyes. Doubt? Insecurity?

"I like seeing you in your element." He gestured toward the books, hoping he sounded sincere and not like he was spouting cheesy pickup lines. "I've never found anything I'm so passionate about the way you are with art."

She sighed, her gaze darting back down to her painting. But she didn't pick up the brush again. "Thanks. It would be nice if passion translated into money."

"Aren't you the one who told me that it's *love* that makes the world go around?" he teased. He was beginning to believe that platitude himself, the more time he spent in Crabtree.

She cleared her throat, then took a swig of

water. "Sometimes, it feels like everything I do, it's not good enough. It's all for nothing."

Gianna's heart pounded. She had no idea why she was telling these things to Dominic, a man who had no business hearing them. All she knew was that she wanted him to know this about her. That she was tired of carrying her insecurities and fears by herself, and that if she shared them with anyone, she thought he might understand the most.

"What do you mean?" His voice rose in disbelief. "Gianna, how can you say that?"

She picked at a fleck of dried paint that had somehow made its way onto the wooden table. "Growing up, I was always compared to my siblings. In school, the teachers would compare my test scores to Estella's, or my athletic ability to Luca's—"

"Wait, I thought Estella was two years younger than you." He frowned.

"She is, but we were in the same classes since she skipped a grade and I started later because I was born in December." She kept pushing her nail against the dried dot of paint, unwilling to look up and meet his gaze. Though she thought she might be able to trust him, another part of her was scared. Scared that he'd see her as weak, incompetent, lacking—all the things she'd been made to feel in school and in her family. "Estella was the smart one, the pretty one, the popular one. She was on the volleyball team and had great grades and the coolest friends. Me? I was always reading a book, and people saw me—I think my family saw me—as someone with her head in the clouds. Someone who knew a lot about fiction but nothing about reality."

She took a deep breath, daring herself to meet his eyes. When she did, they were full of sympathy. He saw her pain, and he cared for her in spite of it. Maybe because of it. That made her chest ache with a sentiment she couldn't discern and gave her the courage to continue.

"I guess that's why my parents want me to work at the restaurant. They don't think I can make it working at Tang's. They believe I'll always need a safety net to catch me. That if I take risks, I'll fail and be disappointed. I know they mean well and they want what's best for me, but sometimes, it feels like they don't believe I can do anything by myself. Like I'll never be as clever as Estella or as hardworking as Luca in their eyes. I'm just..."

"You're *you*, Gianna." He said it like the

mere act of being herself was akin to a comet shooting across the night sky. "How can that not measure up?"

Her hair had slipped from her bun and fallen around her face. Gianna didn't see him lift his arm to put it around her shoulders until he had placed it there. She inhaled deeply, shutting her eyes, breathing in his woodsy scent mingled with spices. She wanted to stay there, wrapped under the shelter of his arm, hearing his steady pulse, forever.

But it was a lie. Dominic wasn't steady, wasn't safe—he couldn't be. Not when it was only a week ago that he'd decided to stick around and give this bookstore thing a go. Not when he could change his mind at any moment. She took a deep breath and separated herself from him. "Thanks."

"You're welcome."

Emmett cleared his throat. "Look, Daddy. Look what I made!"

He held up a sheet of paper with a painting on it. "That's me and Grandma and Grandpa and you and Gianna, having dessert together."

Gianna remained seated as Dominic got up and crossed the room to examine his son's drawing in further detail. As he praised it, marveling at his son's artistic abilities, Gianna couldn't help but wonder. Did she have a place in Dominic's and Emmett's lives? Or would she be forgotten as soon as a second-grader's art project? The thought made her stomach sink.

Chapter Twelve

A week or so after Dominic had shown up outside the bookstore with apology flowers, Gianna found herself smiling and humming to herself as she and Lil made their way to the bowling alley. She'd been so swamped with preparations for the annual fair that she'd almost texted Lillian to cancel their plans. But since she'd paid for a bowling membership at the beginning of the year, she had no financial reason not to go. On top of that, her best friend would have refused to let her do so, or else they would be forfeiting their bowling club's monthly meeting.

Lucky Lane, the venue of their monthly bowling club, was usually quiet the night that they met. All their other club members had bowed out, making various relationship-or baby-related excuses not to be there. It was enough to make a single girl feel lonely, friendless and woefully lacking a romantic partner.

Well, it might have been enough if she wasn't still smiling and humming to herself for no reason, like a lovesick fool. Which was absurd because Gianna was neither foolish nor in love. She had never been in love before—she'd thought she'd been in love with a few high-school crushes. But they'd fizzled out or proven themselves far too unreliable to be a proper love interest. She had no reason to think she was in love now. Especially not with Dominic Tang.

"Gianna, is there a reason you're looking as giddy as a schoolgirl?" Lillian asked her as they walked into Lucky Lane. "Does it have anything to do with a certain bookstore owner?"

"Dominic and I are…getting along," she said, clearing her throat. "That doesn't mean anything."

"Getting along awfully *well*. Well enough for him to bring you flowers, and for you to tuck his son into bed, and for you to hang out with his parents?" asked Lillian with an arched brow.

Her brows were perfectly groomed, which always made Gianna feel inadequate in comparison. While Lillian had long since perfected an everyday makeup look, Gianna had never learned how.

As they walked into the bowling alley, Gianna was surprised to see streamers hung up, loud music playing and bunches of balloons between the lanes.

"Wait, what's happening here? I didn't know there was some kind of event today." Their club picked weeknights because the bowling alley would usually be half-empty then. However, today, there seemed to be dozens of people here, a group of families with their children, and...

Dominic Tang, standing there with one hand on Emmett's shoulder in the lane next to Gianna and Lillian's usual one.

"Ooh, it's Dominic." Lillian nudged her. "But what's all this hullabaloo?"

Gianna choked on a laugh, trying to suppress her amusement at her best friend's use of the word *hullabaloo*. Lillian's old-fashioned vocabulary came courtesy of her grandmother, who was the town's unofficial matchmaker. "I guess we'll find out."

As they walked toward the counter to talk

to the manager, Sam, they heard whooping and hollering from the gathered patrons. Someone had bowled a strike.

"Hi, Sam. I didn't know Lucky Lane was hosting an event today," Lillian said, resting her elbows on the counter. "What's it for?"

Sam, a middle-aged man with a friendly smile and a suspender collection the size of Gianna's bookshelves—today, his suspenders had green and purple polka dots—ran a hand through his thinning hair. "Miss Lillian, so good to see you. And Miss Gianna, your young man there—"

"Whose young man?" Her eyes flew to Lillian.

"Dominic Tang, of course," Sam said cheerily. "He came in earlier today and told me about your situation. Bit of a pickle, that whole AC unit and everything else that happened at the bookstore. So he asked if there was any chance of him setting up some fundraising event where everyone who rents a pair of shoes and a lane can have ten percent of their purchase donated to the bookstore. I figured it wouldn't be bad for either of our businesses and, well, that's why all these people are here. I went into Marchesi's for lunch and told your mom, and she must have gotten the word out. Oh, and he set up a table of some used books that got damaged at the store, and those are selling at a dollar a pop."

"Thanks, Sam," Gianna said, slightly overwhelmed as she tried to process all the information. Dominic had come to the bowling alley and set up an event to raise money for the bookstore? Her heart did a strange flip in her chest. When he'd nonchalantly—or apparently not so nonchalantly—asked her about her evening plans this morning, she'd told him she would be bowling tonight with Lillian.

"Don't worry, ladies. I've saved your usual lane for you." He winked. "And your bowling balls are here, too."

He pointed a finger at their favorite bowling balls. Gianna's was a bright neon yellow with a smiley face drawn on the side, and Lillian's had a floral pattern against an iridescent pink background.

"Wow, it was so nice of Dominic to set all this up," Lillian said, nudging her as they walked toward their usual lane. "Don't you think?"

"It definitely was…" She swallowed, letting Lillian take the first swing. *Nice* didn't quite describe it. *Nice* was holding open the door for a stranger or smiling at a child. This was far more than that. "I didn't expect him to do all this."

Dominic and Emmett were at the lane next to theirs, and when he saw them pass, he looked up and waved.

"Excellent, it's time for me to observe true love in action," Lillian said. "Just let me get this spare…"

Gianna was grateful that her friend was more focused on her bowling strategy than on Dominic. He was concentrating on helping Emmett tie his bowling shoes.

"Yes!" Lillian pumped her fist in the air as her bowling ball knocked into the one remaining pin.

The TV screen above them showed a graphic of the move as Dominic stood and looked up, locking his eyes with hers. "Gianna! I hope I didn't overstep by arranging all this, but I…"

Having just picked up her bowling ball and stepped toward the lane, Gianna waved at him. "Thank you for putting this together."

She then took one step too many, and the slick sole of her bowling shoe made contact with the slippery lane, causing her to careen backward. Gianna dropped the ball onto the lane with a thud and windmilled her arms wildly to keep herself from falling.

"Whoa, are you okay?" Dominic reached for her and placed his hands under her shoulders—not the most graceful way to save someone, but she'd accept it. Gianna heard Emmett run over. She blushed at the thought of the two Tangs seeing her in such an awkward position.

"All…good." She blinked, eyelids fluttering as a wave of dizziness swam over her from the rush of blood to her head. "Thanks for catching me."

Her pulse sped up as Dominic shifted his grip to deposit her onto the bench. Though, it might have been less from the fall and more from the scent of his cologne, that same woodsy, masculine aroma mingling with his gentle touch.

Gianna thought she heard the click of a camera shutter; she looked up to see Lillian pocketing her phone.

"You're supposed to be my best friend, Lil," she managed to say, trying to take deep breaths to slow her racing heart. "I believe one of the key responsibilities of a best friend is to help your friend when they're about to fall to their death in a bowling alley, not take a picture of them in their most life-threatening moments."

"Oh, come on, I've done that before, too, and I didn't die."

She scrunched up her nose as she recalled the moment. "Didn't you have a nasty bruise afterward?"

"Last time I checked, bruises weren't life-threatening." Lillian took a seat on her left, crossing her legs. "I thought you and Dominic looked cute together, so I took a picture."

Emmett sat on the bench next to his father, though he leaned over to look at her, saving her from responding to Lillian's comment. "Hey, look, you bowled a strike!"

She glanced up at the screen. Somehow, despite having nearly sustained a head injury, she had managed to throw the ball in a way that knocked out all the pins in one blow. "Not bad for a girl who almost died."

Dominic frowned. "Are you sure you're all right?"

Gianna wondered how to answer, considering he was still fussing over her like she was a wounded bird, his hand on her shoulder like he worried she would fall over without his touch. She was considering telling him no if he kept hovering over her all night. "Fine. Just fine."

He dropped his hand from her upper arm to hold hers. "Are you sure?"

"Mmm-hmm." She was certain that if she tried to manage actual words, she might make a sound more like a strangled squawk. *Dominic Tang is holding my hand.* It wasn't like she'd never held a man's hand before. And the expression he wore at the moment was one of concern, not love or romantic affection. He was only worried about her.

But his fingers seemed to engulf hers so perfectly, his grip just firm enough to make her feel safe, the warmth of his hand wrapping around hers like a glove.

"That's good." His shoulders relaxed, and he let go of her hand slowly, untangling each finger from hers at a glacial pace. Dominic seemed to realize only then that other people were still in the bowling alley—or maybe that was her imagination, her wishful thinking.

Behind Dominic, she could spy his parents walking toward them with bowling shoes in hand. She waved at them, and Dominic turned around, away from her, as he stood.

"Dad," Emmett said, tugging on the sleeve of Dominic's T-shirt, which read Tang's Terrific Tomes and had a drawing of an open book on the back. "You said you were going to show me how to bowl."

Dominic scratched the back of his neck. "Yes, well, about that…"

"You don't know how to bowl?" Gianna asked him, her arms folded over her chest. She stared up at him as though he'd confessed to hating chocolate or murdering someone. "You arranged all of this at the bowling alley, but you can't *bowl*?"

Lillian tossed her bowling ball between her hands as effortlessly as he would a basketball. "He said he doesn't know how to bowl."

"Still, a grown man, not knowing how to bowl? This is an outrage."

Dominic's parents joined them.

"Grandpa, can you bowl?" Emmett asked.

Dominic's mother responded, picking up a bowling ball. "Back when we were Dominic's age, your grandpa and I were the undisputed champions of our bowling league."

"What does *undisputed* mean?"

"It means no one can argue with it," Dominic's father explained.

"I want to be undisputed, too," Emmett declared.

Dominic chuckled but didn't correct his son. "So, are you going to help us learn how to bowl?"

"Yes, of course." Lillian cleared her throat. "Welcome to Gianna and Lillian's bowling school."

"Let's get the bumpers for them so the ball doesn't roll into the gutter," Gianna suggested.

Half an hour into their "lesson," Dominic felt somewhat more confident about being able to throw a bowling ball without it rolling into the gutter. After forty-five minutes, he felt certain he could hit some pins with it. He'd played basketball in high school but had rarely done any bowling growing up. Being an only child, he hadn't had any siblings to go bowling with, and going with his parents had felt embarrassing and awkward. The last time he'd bowled had been years ago on a date with Carly, at her behest.

He snuck a glance over at Gianna, who was instructing Emmett on how best to grip the bowling ball he carried with both hands. Involuntarily, his lips twitched into a smile. It wasn't simply that she was good with children in general. It was also that she seemed to like Emmett, and his son had warmed up to her.

In Toronto, he'd never entrusted Emmett to any babysitter but the kind neighbor one condo over, a sweet grandmother whose family lived across the country. But here in Crabtree, everything was different. He would have to watch his son grow up. He'd have to let go of him even just that little bit.

Though he'd only known her for a few weeks, Gianna felt like someone he could trust. Even when she was the one who was falling into his arms.

"Are you staring at my best friend?" Lillian's voice interrupted him from his thoughts.

He cleared his throat. "I—"

"It's okay, I don't blame you. She would make a great mom, wouldn't she?" she said, displaying about as much tact as a bull in a china shop. "I think the two of you would make a cute couple. And your son seems to like her."

He narrowed his eyes, trying to understand Lillian's intentions. "Why do you want me to get together with your friend?"

Lillian shrugged. "You spend a lot of time together, and she doesn't want the bookstore to be gutted. Wouldn't it be better for the two of you if, well, you both did the right thing for Crabtree *and* yourselves?"

His shoulders slumped. So, it was about the bookstore again. Gianna didn't care for him. In all likelihood, she'd been irritated by him or felt he had been overstepping when he held her hand. "Right."

Gianna's best friend continued, not seeing the disappointment on his face. "Gianna is an amazing girl, and she needs someone who can appreciate that. You don't seem like a half-bad guy, either, Dominic. You care about your son, and the bookstore, even if you don't show it. I think the two of you would be good for each other."

"Good, how?" he said.

She laughed. "Do you not see it? When you first came back to town, I thought you were a boring, logical businessman who saw everything in black-and-white. But Gianna's not like that. She's more…she has such a strong emotional attachment to Tang's, she would fight you tooth and nail on any idea about changing or gutting the bookstore. But she also… I think she needs someone to ground her. She gets crazy ideas sometimes, and I think she needs someone to tell her that they're not all going to happen. She needs someone to keep her down-to-earth, and I think you'd be able to do that."

He ran a hand through his hair. "Thanks for the insight."

"Anytime." Lillian got up from the bench. "Now, how about you hurry up and bowl, old man? I've been waiting for my turn for five minutes."

He rolled his eyes as he stood up. "I'm only three years older than you and Gianna."

She shrugged. "You are closer to thirty than us, so I think we're allowed to call you *old*."

"Weren't you the one who was just telling me to date Gianna?" he muttered under his breath as he threw the ball.

It curved precariously close to the gutter before knocking out five pins.

Gianna high-fived him as Emmett waited for his ball to roll back toward him on the machine. "Good job. You've improved."

"I had a good teacher." He hadn't felt like flirting with a girl since college. Had it been that long?

He hadn't gone on many dates since Emmett was born. He'd been too busy taking care of him. Then, when his son was in school, he'd been either working or spending time with Emmett. If any of his coworkers—or even teachers at Emmett's school—had tried to gain his attention, he certainly hadn't noticed.

"I'm glad you'll admit it," she said with a grin. "Most men would be too ashamed to say that a woman taught them how to bowl."

Was she flirting back?

He bit his tongue. "I'm not like most men."

"No," she said softly, her gaze scanning him with an expression he couldn't quite identify. "You're most definitely not."

He swallowed thickly, unsure of what to say.

"Thanks for setting all of this up, by the way." She gestured toward the table of books, which was currently being manned by their employee, Garrett, the high-school senior who loved comics and always wore a sci-fi T-shirt. "I didn't expect it when I came in here…but I really appreciate it."

Unbridled gratitude and sincere excitement shone in Gianna's eyes as she glanced at the people milling about the bowling alley and the table of used, damaged books for sale.

"Of course." He shrugged, trying to look cool even as his heart thundered in his chest. "Anything for the bookstore."

Anything to see you smile like that.

"Dad!" Emmett yelled. "Look, I'm bowling backward!"

Dominic stepped back from Gianna, walking over to his son at a pace too fast for his bowling shoes to sustain, skidding across the floor as Emmett did at home in his socks. He made it to the other lane just in time to watch his son throw the ball between his legs with all his might, from a crouching position. He relaxed somewhat, his pulse slowing when he saw Emmett stand upright again, a safe distance from the slippery surface of the lane.

The ball bounced against the polished wood surface, once, then twice, before rolling to a stop and giving a tremendous crash as it knocked out seven of the pins on the left side of the lane.

"That was awesome," he said, high-fiving Emmett. "Maybe this time, if you look where you're throwing, you'll get the other three pins."

"Yeah," his son said, but he wasn't looking at Dominic anymore. Instead, he ran up to Gianna and jumped up and down, grabbing her hands. "Did you see that? Wasn't it cool?"

"It was very cool." Gianna laughed. "Great job, kiddo."

He patted Emmett on the shoulder as he

released Gianna's hands. For a moment, the three of them almost felt…

…like a family.

And it both scared and thrilled him more than he wanted to admit.

Chapter Thirteen

Dominic was surprised to hear himself whistling as he walked from the parking lot toward the bookstore the next morning. He whistled a few off-key bars of some pop song that had been stuck in his head since he'd heard it on the radio.

Trying to remember why he was whistling, however, proved to be a challenge when he saw the car parked in front of Tang's.

He'd recognize it anywhere. The sleek, cherry-red Corvette had been the signature car of his grandfather in his distant youth, and all his subsequent children and grandchildren had begged to own it or just to take it for a spin. He'd always refused when he was alive.

Now that he was dead, though, things had changed.

There was only one man who would be driving Philip Tang's Corvette.

And that was…

"Dominic!" Jack Tang said, leaning against the locked door of Tang's and looking every inch the suave businessman in an expensive suit that probably cost more than the Corvette. "Long time no see, am I right?"

Dominic tried to hide his grimace as he walked up to his older cousin, the twenty-eight-year-old hotshot with an MBA from Wharton who wanted to ensure *everyone* knew his academic credentials. He wanted to say that it hadn't been long enough. But now that he saw Jack standing here, maybe he could ignore their long-standing feud and try to reconcile. "It's good to see you, Jack."

"How's the kid? Where is he? Did you hire a babysitter for him?"

Dominic had the sinking suspicion Jack didn't remember Emmett's name, always calling him "the kid" or "little guy."

"No, he's staying at my parents' place while I work in the store," he said. "What brings you back to town? Last I heard, you were in New York at some fancy Wall Street gig."

"I got bored of that, so I thought I'd come

home and take over the old bookstore. You
don't mind, right?" Jack cast a disparaging eye over the awning of the store. "First
step will be to repaint the whole storefront.
It looks old and worn-out, and who came
up with that name, anyway? I mean, Tang's
Terrific Tomes? That's a mouthful. You want
something that rolls off the tongue."

He decided it was best not to tell Jack that
everyone in town had always referred to the
store as Tang's, since there were bigger fish
to fry. "What do you mean, you're coming
home to take over the bookstore? Ye Ye left
it to me."

"I want proof," Jack said, sticking out his
hand as though he expected everyone to
carry around legal documentation or build-
ing titles in manila envelopes at all times.
"Until then...this store is as much yours as
it is mine."

"It's not *yours* at all," Dominic said, folding
his arms over his chest. "There is nothing in
the will saying you inherited the bookstore.
You weren't even present for the funeral."

He took a deep breath to steady himself.
Their childhood rivalry had begun with the
two of them daring each other to jump into
the lake. Jack had always resented being com-

pared to Dominic growing up. Meanwhile, Dominic had envied how easily his cousin managed to charm people, always getting along with others and making friends within five minutes of meeting them, while Dominic was mostly a loner, aside from his casual friends on the basketball team.

"Neither were you, from what I heard," Jack said, sporting a scowl. However, his expression changed when he spotted Gianna coming down the sidewalk.

Dominic turned to see her; she was wearing a much different outfit from her bowling club T-shirt and jeans last night, now clad in a sunny yellow dress with a teal cardigan. The color pairing made him smile, despite his cousin's irritating presence. "Good morning, Gianna."

"Good morning, Dom—" Her voice cut off when she saw his cousin. "Jack Tang, right?"

"Gianna Marchesi," he said, the tension in his voice belying the pasted-on smile he wore. "Lovely to see you again."

"What are you doing here?" she said, sizing him up like the two of them were in a boxing ring together. It might have been menacing if Gianna weren't five foot three and his cousin five-ten with the build of a hockey player. "I haven't seen you since you left to get your MBA at Wharton and never stopped talking about it."

He didn't know whether to be amused or annoyed by her display of rudeness toward his cousin. Gianna was typically far nicer to him, though he'd admit their second meeting at Marchesi's had shown him a glimpse of her temper.

"While you stayed in this town so you could, what, manage a dying bookstore?" Jack cast another disparaging glance at the storefront. "Did you paint those books yourself because you have no customers and needed to waste your time looking busy?"

"Hey." Dominic edged in front of Gianna, a protective instinct bubbling up inside of him. "Leave her alone. I'm the one who owns this store, so why don't we go somewhere else and talk about your sudden urge to run Tang's?"

Jack yanked on the door handle. "I'll have to take a look at the merchandise."

"No, you won't *have to* do anything, because the store doesn't belong to you," he said.

Gianna cleared her throat. "Jack—"

"It says in the will he left the bookstore to his oldest grandson. Technically, that's me," said Jack, dropping his hand as the door remained shut.

Dominic stepped in front of him with the key. "Allow me."

If Jack wasn't going to leave anytime soon, he'd have to get a tour.

"This is—" Gianna began, but Jack cut her off again.

"Nice windows, good lighting, cute setup. This should be turned into a big chain bookstore. That's the only hope you have of surviving. Nobody buys books in stores anymore. It's all about online shopping. Here's what I'll do with the place—"

"Stop. Talking," Dominic said lowly.

Was this how Gianna had seen him when he'd first returned to Crabtree? A coldhearted, clinical, bloodless businessman who only saw things in dollar signs and profit margins? No wonder she'd disliked him at first.

"Why?" Jack spun on his heels, leaning against a display of books, not caring about the so-called merchandise that he wanted to throw out. "Afraid you'll lose the store if Gianna hears my arguments?"

"The last thing I want to hear is any of your arguments," Gianna said. "If you wanted the family business, you should've gotten a lawyer, not come barging in here like a…a mad-man."

"I didn't come *barging* in here. I waited outside the door for the store to be open," Jack said with a huff. "Anyway. You have one week to convince me that you're the owner of this place. Or else, I'll take you to court and clean you out."

Dominic, slack-jawed and wide-eyed, watched his cousin open the door and slam it shut, toppling a book from a nearby shelf.

"I don't understand," Gianna said, picking up the book that had fallen and reshelving it. "How can he say the bookstore is his? Your grandfather left it to you, didn't he?"

In high school, she'd never liked Jack. He had been a few grades ahead of her, but they'd somehow both ended up in the same summer school English class—her for an advanced level and him because he'd fallen behind—and he'd spent the entire time making rude noises and throwing spitballs at her.

Dominic paced the store. "Grandpa's law-yer interpreted the will to mean that I'm in-heriting it, yes."

"What do you mean, they *interpreted* the will? It's a will, not a constitution. How could it be *mis*interpreted?" she said, her brows furrowing. Her heart pounded at the possibilities. What if Dominic decided he didn't want the bookstore? What if he'd only been defending her to be polite? What if he seized the opportunity to let Jack have the store?

"He said the store would go to his oldest grandson. Jack is older than me by a few months. However, technically, Jack isn't his grandson since his mother had him with another man who died before she married my uncle," he explained.

Gianna frowned. Her fingers dug into her skin as she folded her arms across her chest. "That doesn't seem fair. Philip Tang wasn't the kind of man to do that."

"No, but maybe he…maybe he thought Jack would be off in the big city after getting his MBA, doing great things like working on Wall Street. He never wanted to stay in Crabtree." Dominic looked thoughtful. Nostalgic. Almost sad.

"Did *you* want to stay in Crabtree back then?" she probed. *God, please, I don't want him to say no. Not just because of what it would mean for the store.*

Because I want him and Emmett to stay.

Because I love having them in my life, and

I don't want them to go. Even if it's selfish of me to ask, Lord, please...

Let him want to stay.

Dominic stopped pacing, his shoe catching on a snag in the carpet and causing him to stagger slightly. "Yes and no."

She hopped up on the counter, legs dangling off of it, so that she could be eye level with him. "Yes and no?"

"I wanted to stay in Crabtree with Carly and raise Emmett together. But she wanted other things. After that, it was too painful to go around town and see all the places we had been together, all the things we had done together and all the people we both knew. I didn't want anyone's pity or judgment. So it was far easier to leave. But I never meant to stay away so long. I guess I got used to being on my own."

She couldn't imagine moving to another city, away from her entire family and all her friends, away from the church they all attended and the only support system she had ever known. "Did you ever get lonely?"

"All the time, but..." He sighed. "I didn't want to bring anyone else into our lives. Mine and Emmett's. I guess I didn't feel like there was anyone else I could trust."

"Why do you think your grandpa left you the bookstore?" she asked him.

The question snapped him out of his trance. "I...we should go to his house. He left me a key to his house, and since I've been back, I've never once gone. Come on, let's go there after your shift ends. I'm sure we can find something to prove who the bookstore belongs to."

Gianna tilted her head to one side as she hopped off the counter. "He didn't give a key to Jack?"

"I hope not..." Dominic shook his head, his face suddenly animated. Passionate. "If he did, well, I'd be upset."

"You care about the bookstore now, don't you?" She tried to suppress her grin, fearing she would look smug. "And here I thought you wanted to get rid of it."

"I care a lot about the bookstore..." He looked at her with his deep brown eyes, which held an expression she couldn't quite read. But if she had to guess, she would say it was something like...affection. "And the people working in it."

Just then, the door swung open and the bell jingled. "Be there in a minute!"

While she usually enjoyed the day-to-day

work of running the bookstore, and perhaps more so now that Dominic was working with her, today her shift seemed to drag on forever. She triangulated her gaze between the watch on her wrist, the grandfather clock steadily ticking on the wall and her phone's clock. At four, she eagerly handed over responsibilities to Garrett. Then, she hopped into Dominic's car, and they drove to Philip Tang's house.

Gianna had always thought it would be almost disrespectful to enter a home where someone had died, especially someone whom she had known as well as Gianna had known Philip. However, rather than feeling like she was in a shrine or a museum dedicated to the memory of the kind old man, she felt more like a detective looking for clues. She found clues of a life well lived. There were framed family pictures on the wall and a little height chart with the letters *D* and *J* scrawled above it, which she assumed stood for *Dominic* and *Jack*. Despite the unpleasant encounter with Jack that morning, it made her smile to think of the two men as little boys, competing with each other.

The walls were painted a warm yellow. Dominic paused in the entryway when he saw it. "I knew your dress reminded me of something. It's the exact color of these walls. I used to come here all the time as a kid, and…"

He flushed slightly. She let him trail off, not wanting to embarrass him, but cherished the words and their implications like a treasure. "So, where's his office? I assume that's where he would keep important files and stuff, right?"

He hadn't always been the most organized, especially in his old age, but Gianna hoped he would have remembered the important things. That was how it had always been with him; he'd lose his keys but never forget any of his employees' birthdays. Philip Tang would wear his sweater turned inside out, but always remember to ask after her siblings and family. He was forgetful, but he had been so heart-achingly *good*.

"Yeah," Dominic said, his voice sounding distant. He trailed his fingers over the leather sofa, covered by a yellow afghan, and drew them away with a faint layer of dust. "It's so weird being here after all this time… I've missed so much. Too much."

Was it her imagination, or did his voice crack on the last two words?

"It's funny how much we don't realize what we're missing until we go back," she said, thinking suddenly of all the times she'd vowed to leave Marchesi's and never look back, yet always found herself drawn toward the family business again in times of crisis or celebration.

"Anyway." Dominic straightened. "To the office we go."

They walked down the hall and cracked open a mahogany door. It revealed a room overflowing with boxes of files, stacks of paper and several filing cabinets, one of which Dominic shoved to prop open the door.

"Wow." She'd known Philip Tang was disorganized, but she hadn't known he was *this* disorganized. "Are you sure you want to do this? Seems like there's a lifetime's worth of paper cuts waiting in this room."

"I'm sure it's more like...organized chaos. There has to be *some* method to his madness," said Dominic, though it sounded more like a hopeful suggestion than a certain statement.

In the center of the desk, surrounded by stacks of manila folders, was a well-worn Bible, leather-bound with a cracked, peeling spine. Gianna carefully maneuvered around the mess and picked it up.

The front cover fell open, revealing an inscription on the yellowed pages. She passed it to Dominic, feeling like she was violating his family's privacy.

He read it aloud, allowing her to feel better about what was essentially snooping around a dead man's house. Though she'd originally considered it morally approved, considering she was with the aforementioned man's grandson, she was now having second thoughts.

"'To my beloved Rachel, on the day of our wedding,'" he read aloud. "'May your love for the Lord grow, and increase our love for each other all the years of our life.' Wow. I knew they had a great marriage. I mean, it lasted thirty years, until my grandmother passed, but..."

She peeked over his shoulder, reading the spidery script. "That's sweet. The kind of thing everyone should aspire to. It's a shame most people don't attain it."

She meant every word. Most relationships she saw were based on physical appearances or superficial ideas of compatibility, rather than deeply rooted in the love of God. That was what she wanted for her future husband, and she wondered if Dominic felt the same.

He shut the Bible gently and placed it back

on the desk. "Yeah. I'd love for my—for Emmett to see the same thing from his parents. It's a shame it never worked out."

His voice was tight. She reached out and gripped his hand. "It doesn't necessarily have to be that way. Just because things didn't work out with his biological mother doesn't mean…"

What was she saying? Was she offering something he didn't want?

"…doesn't mean you can't start over with someone else," she finished.

He shook his head. "Emmett's never known his mom. I think being here, in Crabtree, it's been great for him to get that from his grandma, but it's not the same."

"Would you ever remarry?" she said, unsure if she was stepping on uneven ground, saying things she would later regret, about to be sucked into a quicksand of fraught emotions.

"If I found the right woman, I'd marry her in a heartbeat."

He'd marry her in a heartbeat. Not *her*. This imaginary, ideal woman didn't exist. Because if she did exist, he would have married her already, and he'd had nearly a decade to find her.

Dominic's fingers tightened around hers. "What about you, Gianna?"

"What about me?" she asked, keeping her gaze fixed on the wobbly stacks of paperwork on Philip Tang's cherrywood desk. "I'm not looking for anybody."

"But if you were?" Did he sound…hopeful? Was she reading things into his voice, into this moment, that didn't exist?

"I'd look for a man who…" She cleared her throat, trying to decipher the scrawled words on one of the sheets. "A man who's proven that he's reliable and steady, who can be a support in my life, not someone unstable who might pack up and leave at any time. A man who can be my anchor when I feel like I'm drifting. Someone whom I can lean on, and someone whom I respect and help when he needs it. Someone who isn't afraid to admit when he's wrong."

His thumb brushed over the back of her hand, whisper soft, so gentle yet so steadying that it tethered her to this instant. No matter what else she tried to think of, she could focus only on him. At this very moment of her life, holding Dominic's hand, talking about everything she might want in a husband, she realized that he might just be all of those things.

Chapter Fourteen

Three hours later, Dominic was still combing through the numerous files and boxes of paperwork scattered around his grandfather's study. Gianna had gone home after two hours, saying she had to work on something related to the fair. Despite her help, he'd only managed to sort through a fraction of the items, determining that most of them were either tax-related documents, family photo albums or inventories of the bookstore. They were all covered in his grandfather's handwriting, which seemed to have grown increasingly messy as he aged because some of the newer files were barely legible.

Finally, after the sixth paper cut, he moved a box aside and sat in his grandfather's leather chair.

"Ye Ye." He used the Chinese term for paternal grandfather, holding his head in his hands and shutting his eyes. "Why did you want me to have the store? Or did you want Jack to take it and run it like a bookstore with no heart and no soul? Did you want it to succeed as a business? Or did you want it to be a place where people come to gather, to join with their friends and family, to be the center of the town?"

He spoke the words aloud, talking to nobody and yet feeling like his grandfather might be present in the room, sitting across from him. He could see him now, smiling the same patient and wise smile he had always worn when Dominic had asked him for help with a math problem or a family argument. He'd never lectured him, instead giving cryptic proverbs that later proved to be useful when he took the time to sit down and think about them. Which was probably the whole point. His grandfather had wanted him to think for himself and to be gently guided in the right direction, not dragged on a leash.

The doorbell rang. He frowned, wondering if it was Gianna, back because she'd forgotten something. He got up and walked toward the door, only to find… "Luca?"

"I heard you might need help moving things," Luca said, wearing a pair of worn work gloves. "Gianna called me."

Dominic frowned. "I thought you'd be busy at Marchesi's."

"You know, Dom, it's like you don't want me around or something." Luca kicked off his shoes and began walking into the house. He'd always been the type to ask for forgiveness rather than permission. "The restaurant will survive without me for one night."

Dominic shook his head, trying to clear away his surprise and replace it with gratitude. "I'm glad to have your help. The office is this way."

He and Luca managed to shift the boxes, filing cabinets and crates around the room into a more manageable workspace, and both of them were soon leafing through the files, Dominic with renewed vigor.

"Thanks for coming, Luca." He began sorting through some folders that looked like they were all irrelevant to their search. Still, maybe there would be something useful there. "You didn't have to."

"You're still my friend, Dom. I wish we'd kept in touch after everything… You left so suddenly, I thought you didn't want to see any of us anymore, even your parents." Luca shifted a box on top of another one with a grunt.

"That's not true," he said automatically, but realized it was just a polite defense mechanism. "After Carly… I mean, we'd just had Emmett, and a few months later, she left us. I felt like a fool, and I definitely didn't want to face all the people who'd told me that I was rushing into things with her. But you've still been a good friend."

Luca sighed. "Maybe. Maybe not. I did try to warn you away from Gianna."

He shifted his weight. He still wasn't certain whether to stay here, or what his feelings for Gianna were. All he knew was he wanted to find out. "You were right to do that. I was pretty unsure of myself and my next steps when I first got to town, and it would've been wrong to let anyone get too close just to leave again."

"Thanks for saying I'm right. You never did when we were seventeen." Luca snickered. "Here, help me move this stuff off the desk."

They swept the things from his grandfather's desk into an empty cardboard box, accidentally knocking his Bible to the floor.

Dominic picked up the tome that had fallen to the ground. A folded piece of paper rested under it. He unfolded it, wondering what it could be that Philip Tang had left in it. A love letter to his wife, perhaps?

"What's that?" Luca said, looking over at him.

"Some kind of letter." As he deciphered his grandfather's handwriting, he saw that it was addressed to him.

Dear Dominic,

I don't know where you'll be by the time you read this. I hope you are back where you belong.

I left the bookstore to you. I want you to have it and take good care of it. Gianna Marchesi is already doing a great job of taking care of it, but together, I hope the two of you can make it even better.

The bookstore is yours. Every piece of Tang's should belong to you. Tell my lawyer to be less cryptic the next time he's drafting a will. I gave him your name, yet he's forgotten to put it in, only writing "oldest grandson." This store is my gift to you. Consider it a fresh start. You can do whatever you want with it,

but I hope you'll not only keep it in business but preserve its heart and soul.
All my love,
Your grandfather, Philip Tang

Dominic found himself brushing away a tear as he read and reread the letter, soaking in each word as they warmed his heart. His grandfather had not only given Dominic the store but also so much more. A lifetime of wisdom packed into the cramped handwriting on the small page, slightly smudged in some areas. He quickly refolded it as he picked up a tissue and blew his nose.

Sitting down on the desk, the only empty surface in the room, he tucked the letter into the pocket of his shirt. "I guess I'm staying."

Luca jumped up from his crouching position and clapped him on the back. "I'm so happy to hear that, man!"

He missed his grandfather terribly. But now he had his marching orders. Dominic would stay here and do the work his grandfather—and God—had seen fit to give him.

"Gianna, you've been spending an awful lot of time with Dominic Tang recently," her mother said, apropos of nothing.

She set down the dish she had been wash-ing, placing it into the top rack of the dish-washer. "Is there a point you're trying to make? Come out and say it, Mom."

"Gianna, there's no need to be so defen-sive." Her mother hummed to herself a line from an old Cantonese opera as she brought more empty plates from the dining table into the kitchen. "I was only making conversa-tion."

She sighed. Her mother frequently started conversations with innocent-sounding state-ments that turned into arguments. Or worse, lectures. "I enjoy Dominic's company, and he *is* the new owner of Tang's."

"That he is," her mother said cryptically as she packed away the leftover fried rice into a glass container. "How's his son?"

"Emmett is…" She smiled at the thought of him. "He's very rambunctious but sweet. A little wild, but all young boys are at his age. Like Luca was, though a tad more bookish."

"Hmm." Whenever Nancy Marchesi com-municated in wordless syllables, it never boded well for her children.

Gianna dropped the sponge into the sink and took off her rubber gloves. "What is it?"

"Nothing."

"Mama, don't insult my intelligence." She put the gloves back on and picked up the sponge again just to have something to do with her hands.

"Dear, I would never do that."

"Okay, then please, tell me what you think I'm doing wrong." She knew her mother wouldn't stop with the passive-aggressive comments until she had said what she needed to—or at the very least, until she had dropped her hints in thinly masked snide remarks and jabs.

"I don't think *you're* doing anything wrong per se, Gianna... Wait, are you using the sponge? It would be a lot more efficient to use steel wool on that."

"I thought you said I wasn't doing anything wrong," she tried to joke as she picked up the steel wool pad to scrub at a nasty baked-in cheese stain on the pan.

"Anyway, my point is, I want you to be careful."

"Careful when I'm doing the dishes?"

"No, no, careful about Dominic Tang. Just because he's good-looking doesn't mean he's a good guy, you know."

"Mom, if you're talking about his past, that was seven years ago." She scrubbed harder at the stain, frustrated when the spot refused to budge. She added more dish soap.

"It doesn't change the fact that he hasn't made a decision about whether to stay in Crabtree or not. You don't want to be strung along by a man who's seeing his time here as some little blip in his life before he jets back to Toronto."

Was that how he saw her and the bookstore? As just a break from real life? Nothing more than a distraction from what was actually important?

Gianna took a deep breath, her arm burning as she scoured the pan. "I'm just friends with Dominic, so I don't know why you're saying all these things, anyway."

"If you were only friends, you wouldn't be so upset with me right now, Gianna." Her mother patted her on the shoulder. Her sweet perfume suddenly smelled too cloying.

"I'm not... My relationship with Dominic is all about the bookstore." A soapy bubble floated up and popped in midair. She glanced down at the pan. It was clean now. Scratched, but clean. "I love the bookstore. I'd be working there whether or not Dominic owned it."

"And just a few weeks ago, you might have been left with no job if he had decided to gut the place. The last thing you want, honey, is to be attached to a man who hasn't made up his mind."

With those words, her mother dropped a kiss on Gianna's cheek and left the kitchen.

Gianna finished washing the rest of the dishes in silence, contemplating her mother's words. She knew her mom was right and only wanted the best for her, but did she have to get her point across the way she did? It always felt like her mother wanted to undermine her decisions and make her question her own judgment. Though she knew her mother wanted her to be in a job that had good stability and to be in a relationship with a man who wasn't prone to leave at any moment…

Hadn't she had the same thought earlier in the day?

Gianna untied the apron from her waist and grabbed her purse and keys. She bid her father and siblings good-night and said a quick good-bye to her mom before heading out the door of the Marchesi home. Framed family pictures lined the foyer: the three of them as children, Luca at a basketball game holding up a trophy, Gianna at a spelling bee with a wide, gap-toothed grin, Estella at a gymnastics meet. Their parents had poured their hearts and souls into their children and the restaurant.

She knew all they wanted was for their children to have a life that was stable. Grounded. Certain.

And that was why she got into her car and drove to Dominic Tang's house to tell him that whatever was between them couldn't continue. Because she knew he was uncertain, drifting and unmoored, and she needed someone who could be her anchor. She wanted a man who would love her as Christ did, and if he was going to leave in a few weeks, Dominic wasn't for her.

Perhaps he had decided to keep the store. But that didn't mean he had decided to stay in Crabtree.

And she didn't think her heart could bear it if he left.

Chapter Fifteen

Dominic finished eating dinner with Emmett. His mother was off at knitting club, and his father had gone to play a friendly round of mini golf with his buddies—he was still surprised his father had taken *that* up as a hobby after retirement—and they were washing up when the doorbell rang.

"I wanna get it," Emmett declared, running at breakneck speed toward the door. He almost knocked a plate into the sink as he set down his dishes.

"No running in the house," he said.

Emmett's footsteps immediately slowed to a more sedate pace. "If I walk, can I get the door?"

He sighed and followed him there. "Go ahead."

When his son opened the door, he heard someone say, "Hi, Emmett. Is your father home?"

His heart leaped. *Gianna.*

He nearly ran toward the front door before reminding himself to set a good example for Emmett.

"Dominic," Gianna said when she saw him. She managed a weak smile. He frowned. Had something happened to the store? Was it Jack?

"Come in," he said, taking her light coat from her and hanging it up. "Can I get you anything? Tea, coffee, water?"

"Some water, please," she said. "But I can get it my—no, it's fine. I don't need anything."

He frowned. Something must be dreadfully wrong. "Are you sure?"

She nodded, looking too tense to speak.

Dominic crouched down to look Emmett in the eye. "Why don't you go upstairs and read in your room? Me and Gianna are going to talk."

"That's *Gianna and I*," his son said immediately.

He chuckled. "I know. I was just testing you."

"Okay, Dad. See you, Gianna!" Emmett ran upstairs.

"Let's go into the living room," he suggested. "What's the matter? Is it about the store? Is it Jack? Did he come by again to harass you?"

Gianna shook her head. "No, I…it's not about Jack."

He led her toward the love seat where his parents always sat. "Take a seat."

"Well, it's…" Her eyes darted around the room, and they landed on the piece of paper sticking out of the pocket of his button-down shirt. "What's that?"

"A letter from my grandfather. I found it in his house." He pulled it out, unfolding it, and before he knew what he was doing, he extended it to her. "Do you want to read it?"

She gave a brief nod and took it from him. As Gianna's eyes skimmed over the page, he watched her expressions, taking in her wistful smile, which morphed into a gentle laugh as she read something she must have found particularly funny, before she paused. "Why would he mention me in a letter to you?"

"Keep reading, and I suppose you'll find out," he said, his fingers tightening, nails digging into his palms; he forced himself to uncoil, to stop leaning toward her, almost falling out of his chair in anticipation of what she might say.

Finally, she finished reading the letter and passed it back to him. "Wow. So, um, what did you decide?"

He took a deep breath. What he said next felt perfectly right. "I'm staying in Crabtree."

What he didn't expect was Gianna leaping out of her seat and flinging her arms around him. "That's great! Dom, I'm so happy to hear that."

His eyes narrowed as they met hers. "You've never called me that before."

"Oh, sorry, I... I mean, Luca calls you that."

"You're not your brother." A fact he was acutely aware of when she was in his arms, her hair tickling his cheek and her small hand on his shoulder. Dominic patted her on the back before easing into the hug, uncertain of how to respond. "Wait, what did you come here to talk to me about?"

"It's nothing important. Just a silly thought I had. I've forgotten it now."

His brows furrowed. "Really? It must have been important that you drove all the way here instead of picking up the phone."

"No, no... I guess I wanted to see you in

person." Her arms were still around him, and he found he didn't mind one bit. If he was being honest, he hadn't hugged anyone other than Emmett and his mother in a long time, and neither of those embraces had lasted this long or made him feel…

Well, he wasn't sure *how* he felt, only that he never wanted to let go of Gianna Marchesi. At least, not for a long time.

He smiled, his hand still on her back, his fingers tangling in the strands of her hair, which she'd taken out of her braid and now wore loosely over her shoulders. "I'm glad you came because I wanted to see you, too."

Dominic heard her breath hitch. "You did?"

"Yes." He gazed down at her, and as her eyes softened, her expression adoring as she looked up at him…he thought she might feel the same way.

He pulled her closer and leaned down to kiss her.

Gianna Marchesi tasted like chocolate and oranges, two things that should have been too sweet together, yet were the perfect combination. This kiss felt like the perfect culmination of a lifetime. A lifetime of waiting, of hoping, of knowing what he was longing for but not knowing who to find it in.

Her hands grasped his shoulders, and she kissed him back. God had brought him here. Not just to Crabtree, not just to the bookstore, but to her. To Gianna.

"Wow," she said softly when he pulled away. "That was…"

His heart skidded, his pulse like a record scratch. "Was that too much? I—"

"No, it was…" Her smile was less teasing, her expression dazed, as though she were in another world. "It was just right."

He grinned. "I thought so, too."

"So, what was it about the letter that made you decide to stay?" Gianna asked, her heartbeat still running a marathon, her face still feeling flushed, as though she were glowing with a light from within. She was sitting next to Dominic on the sofa.

"Well, you know I've been living on my own with Emmett for so long…" he began.

"Yes. I know."

"I suppose during that time I didn't want to come back to Crabtree, not just because I thought people would gossip about me and Carly."

"Where is Carly now?" she said before she could stop herself. He was about to open up to her, and she ruined it by asking about his ex-fiancée, who had left him. *Great going, Gianna.*

"I actually don't know," he said. "I haven't been in touch with her since she took off her ring and left us."

She unwound slightly, relaxing against him. "Sorry for asking. I was only curious."

"I know you didn't mean any harm by it. There's no need to apologize. I'd be curious too if I were you," he said. "Anyway, as I said, I didn't only stay away from Crabtree because of the scandal of it all."

She smiled at his dramatic delivery of the last few words.

"I stayed away because…after Carly left me, I was scared of having to rely on anyone else when they could just up and leave me so easily. If she could leave—the mother of my child, the girl I thought I was going to be with for the rest of my life—then…then I guess I thought anyone could abandon me." His voice cracked. They both stared at the roaring fireplace, a fire burning even in the balmy climes of early summer. "If there was something so *wrong* with what I wanted, with who I was, then I couldn't possibly love anyone else or be loved in return."

"Dominic," she said, because what else could she say? There was nothing that could take away the pain of the last seven years, or immediately transform the beliefs he'd carried with him since that event. But maybe she could be there for him. Maybe she could comfort him in his pain and carry a little bit of it for him. "That isn't true."

He sighed. "I know that now. After I found God, when a coworker invited me to a Bible study, I knew that He wasn't punishing me for my sins by having Carly leave me."

"I thought you were…" She wasn't sure what she had believed about his faith.

He must have read the confusion in her tone because he continued, "I had been raised Christian but never took it seriously. Church was just another activity for me. I wish I'd listened to my grandfather more whenever he tried to talk to me about God, but then… I suppose Emmett wouldn't be here now."

"I'm glad you have Emmett," she said, leaning closer to him.

"Me, too," he said, and even in the dark, she could hear the smile in his voice. "I'm glad I have you, as well."

"Finish the story." She nudged him, her elbow lightly tapping his side.

"I want to stay in Crabtree, not because I'm tired of being lonely, but because I'm tired of pretending I can do everything on my own."

"So, what are you going to do?" She tried not to hold her breath, butterflies fluttering in her stomach as she awaited his response.

"I decided I'm going to fight for the bookstore, and you're going to help me."

Chapter Sixteen

On the drive back home, Gianna found herself consumed by thoughts of what had transpired at Dominic's parents' house. Not simply the kiss, though *that* was exciting enough to occupy an hour-long phone call with Lillian. No, it was what he had said.

If Dominic could change—if he could change his heart, if *God* could change his heart about the bookstore and about staying in Crabtree—then who was she to believe *she* couldn't change? Before he had come into town, Gianna had thought herself perfectly content with her life. She had a wonderful job, a loving—if overbearing and rowdy—family and great friends.

But there had been something missing. Not simply a romantic relationship, but something deeper. *Purpose*. Gianna had always felt like she was missing something. Growing up, she'd thought it was because she always felt overlooked by her parents. Alberto and Nancy Marchesi had always been so occupied with running a business and shepherding their three children to sporting events or extracurricular activities that they could never be bothered to pay close attention to the inner workings of each of their children. Not that anyone could blame them. Some days, it had been a blessing that the three of them all managed to get dressed and arrive at school on time. Weekends had been filled with Luca's basketball games or Estella's piano recitals or even Gianna's spelling bees, if they weren't already booked with large Marchesi family gatherings.

There had been so much *stuff* happening that Gianna had never given any thought to what she wanted to do in her life until she graduated high school and was left holding a diploma and her heart in her hands. Both her siblings were more than happy to go into the family business, but Gianna had never felt the same way. Being in the kitchen all day was drudgery; serving customers felt enjoyable but mind-numbing, especially in a restaurant that was always jam-packed with Crabtree's townspeople. She wanted to be…well, a selfish part of her wanted to stand out.

She wanted to be more than another Marchesi in a small town full of them. Gianna had wanted to blaze her own trail and chart her own course. But she'd had no idea how to do that until one day, while at the store, Philip Tang had remarked that she spent so much time at the bookstore, she might as well get paid to do it. That had been the beginning of her career, in which she'd risen the ranks from shelf-stocker to cashier to, finally, store manager.

She had found each second of it to be entertaining. It was, for starters, a change of scenery. Gianna loved books, which made her job a lot easier. She enjoyed reading to the children whenever they came into the store and helping someone pick out the perfect book when they weren't sure what they wanted to read. She even loved reshelving books after they had been pulled out of place.

But did she feel fulfilled? Did she feel like she had found her calling? What had she been seeking from the bookstore, and why couldn't it satisfy her? Was it because what she'd been looking for after all wasn't a job, but approval?

Gianna parked in the driveway in front

of the bungalow she shared with three other housemates but made no motion to go inside or even to get out of the car. She shut off the ignition and simply sat there, thinking.

Suddenly, her phone rang in the cup holder, jolting her out of her reverie. She grabbed it, swiping at the screen to answer. Who would be calling her so late?

"Hello?"

"Gianna, it's me," her mother said, the way she always did, knowing—or just assuming—her children would immediately recognize her voice. Which, of course, Gianna did. "I was just calling to say…"

"Yeah, Mom?" She took a deep breath, steeling herself for her mother's next words. What would it be this time? Another lecture on why she ought to stay away from Dominic? Another talk about keeping her distance from the man who'd just kissed her? "What is it?"

"I wanted to tell you, after our last conversation, that I love you." Even through her cell phone, she could picture her mother's gentle smile, that patient, weary, but ever-loving smile, and it softened Gianna's defenses, which had been on guard to shield against any attack. "I love you, even when I don't agree with you."

"I love you, too, Mom." She rested her cheek against the cool glass of the window as spring rain began to fall against the windshield. "I know you care about me."

It wasn't that they had different goals, more like competing visions of the same goal. Her mother wanted what was best for her children, but her perspective was grounded in a certain experience that Gianna would never have. Unlike her mother, Gianna hadn't married her high-school sweetheart and promptly started a restaurant, then had three children with him.

"Oh, honey." Her mother sighed. "I don't want you to look back in life and have any regrets about who you married or the path you've taken. That's all. I want to protect you, but you're not a little girl anymore."

Gianna traced her fingertips along the trail a raindrop was making down her window. "I know, Mom. I'm an adult now."

And she had a distinct feeling that if she let Dominic slip away, she *would* regret it.

"I'll always love you, no matter what. You *do* know that, don't you?"

Gianna paused, watching the rain slide down the car's windshield. *Did* she know that?

Or had she been spending her time wondering if she needed to do a little more, to work a little harder to be loved? Wondering if she needed to be a little *better* to be loved—better than her siblings, better than who she'd been, better than the image of herself that she thought her parents had?

Even when she'd been working summer shifts at Marchesi's, her parents had still loved her. She'd known they had. When she'd stayed up late to do her math homework and turned it in at the last minute in exchange for a C, her mother had simply patted her on the head and said that she knew Gianna could do better next time. They'd still loved her unconditionally, no matter what she accomplished.

All this time, Gianna had thought she needed to be special to be loved. She'd thought she needed to go out there and achieve something lasting, to revamp a bookstore or paint books or win the town's annual fair. But she didn't.

She didn't have to do any of those things. God loved her enough. If He could do that, then surely she could trust that her parents could, no matter what she did or didn't do to earn their approval.

Surely, she could trust that they loved her still.

"Gianna?" her mom said. "You know that, right?"

A tear trickled down her face, and she swiped her cheek, holding back a sob. "I know, and I'll always love you, too. I'm gonna go to bed soon, okay?"

"Good, good. Don't stay up too late, sweetie. Good night."

She echoed her mom's parting line before hanging up.

Her mother had only wanted to protect Gianna. That was all she'd ever wanted. She wasn't overlooked by her mother. She was loved by her.

And for the first time in a while, Gianna smiled while tears cascaded down her face.

Maybe she *would* teach Emmett how to make baked risotto, after all.

Chapter Seventeen

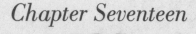

Gianna and Lillian sat across from each other on the Chengs' living room floor. During their usual get-togethers, they'd watch movies, eat popcorn and generally catch up on their lives. Thus, this time was unusual since they were technically working. Being the daughter of the fair's organizer, Lillian had been delegated several tasks by her mother during her weekend away. She had to organize the layout of the carnival's booths, ensure that all decorations and entries matched the theme and make sure everyone had submitted the proper paperwork to be able to set up their respective booths.

Gianna had just put the finishing touches on one of her painted books and had spread newspapers on the floor to keep paint from getting on the hardwood.

"I don't know if it's ethical for me to work on this carnival thing with you, Lil. Technically, I'm a participant, so wouldn't I be accused of helping myself and giving my booth a prime spot?" she said as Lillian pulled out a map of the fairground.

"Nonsense. My mother will check my work to make sure everything is fair and impartial."

"By 'checking your work,' you mean she'll just redo everything to her liking?" Gianna said.

"Yes, so I don't know why she asked me to do these things for her."

"Maybe she's finally loosening up," Gianna suggested. They both considered the thought before erupting into a fit of laughter.

Lillian unrolled the map on the coffee table, standing over its laminated surface with several colorful magnets and two dry-erase markers. She handed one to Gianna. "Where do you want your booth to go?"

"Lil, I don't need to get first pick. As I said, it's unfair—"

"Gianna, I want you guys to win. You're my best friend. Also, wouldn't it be nice if you guys won the fair and you could prove to Dominic that it was a good idea for him to stay, even without the letter?"

She sighed. It was true that part of her *did* want to prove to Dominic that staying was the best decision, with or without their kiss and his grandfather's letter, but she didn't want to rig the carnival to do it. Gianna marked a *T* for where she wanted Tang's to go. "There."

"Hmm." Lillian cocked her head to one side. "Let's see… Close to the judges' table, but not so close that they'll notice if something goes wrong. You're pretty close to the bathrooms, too, but far enough that it doesn't smell bad, and you'll have a nice mix of shade and sun. Excellent choice."

"I knew you'd approve." In truth, she had just marked down a random spot on the map and hoped for the best.

"Now, let's decide where everyone else's booths should go." Lillian read off the list of booths. "Ooh, Dominic's mom is entering with an egg tart booth."

Every year, there were three distinct types of booths and three groups of judges. One group judged the quality of the food, and thus went around taste-testing every pie, cake, sandwich and whatever else had been cooked or baked. Another judged the quality of the goods sold by the contestants—everything from hand-knit sweaters to hand-thrown pottery to handmade jewelry. Finally, the third group of judges would evaluate the activities offered by other booths: dunking for apples, fishing for plastic goldfish or shooting hoops. Gianna and Dominic's booth would fall into the second category, since their small business was selling hand-painted books.

"Her pie is pretty good."

"Good, because you'll have to learn how to make her recipe, as her future daughter-in—"

"Oh, come on, Lillian, don't tell me you're already planning my wedding."

Though she had no doubt that her best friend would be an excellent wedding planner, she also had no romantic ideas about what might happen between her and Dominic. It was better not to let herself dream and be disappointed, than fall headfirst only to find herself without a parachute.

"As your best friend and maid of honor, I simply must do so." Lillian put a kitschy pie-shaped fridge magnet next to Gianna's marker on the map. "Here, you guys can be next to each other."

"Okay." Gianna shook her head at her friend's antics. "What about Mrs. Jenkins's crafts?"

They focused on the task at hand in earnest

and began planning the carnival layout with an efficiency that Lillian's mother would be proud of.

Gianna only prayed it would go off without a hitch. And, if she was going to be completely truthful, she prayed she and Dominic would win in at least one of the categories.

It would go a long way in helping the store with its financial issues.

"What are all the prize categories this year? Are they the same as last year's?" she asked Lillian.

"Let's see." Lillian pulled up a list on her phone. "There's the prize for the small business that's done the most for the community, the prize for the most creative or innovative business idea, the prize for best baked goods and the prize for the most beautifully decorated booth."

She chewed on her lower lip as Lillian went on to describe the different prizes for each award; they were listed in descending order, ranging from fifteen thousand to one thousand. What were the odds that they would win? "Do you think Tang's has a shot at any of them?"

"As your best friend, I'm obligated to tell you that you have a shot at all of them, even the baked goods. As someone who's seen a *lot* of the entries, I'll have to tell you that someone else will likely win the most innovative business idea. You wouldn't believe all the new inventions and patents for everything from hiking accessories to farming equipment." She shook her head. "I mean, how many Taber corn farmers can there even *be* passing through Crabtree? And don't even get me started on the little outfits for the Gopher Hole Museum."

Gianna giggled at the mention of the Gopher Hole, a tourist attraction in their province that was both adorable and extremely eccentric. "There must be a market for those things if people are selling them at the fair."

"Don't worry. You're bound to win *something*," Lil said, which sounded like a reassuring consolation prize for not catering to corn farmers and gopher exhibits.

"That's exactly what I wanted to hear." Gianna picked up the book she'd finished decorating and stared at it. She began peeling the pages apart, feeling, rather than seeing, the small ridges of paint as she carefully separated them so they wouldn't clump together as they dried. "What booth are you most excited for?"

"Definitely Mrs. Tang's egg tart and pie booth... I mean, have you tasted her egg tarts?" Lillian sighed. "Perfection."

Gianna peeled back another page. "Emmett said that was his favorite, too."

"You're spending an awful lot of time with Dominic and Emmett for someone who doesn't want me to plan your wedding," Lillian said in a singsong tone, nudging her.

Rolling her eyes, she finished separating the last of the pages. "I do work with the man."

"It's okay, Gianna. You can admit there's more to it than work."

Could she, though? He'd said he'd stay and fight for the bookstore with her.

He hadn't promised there'd be anything more than that.

Wiping a bead of sweat off her forehead, Gianna riffled through the stack of receipts in the cash register. Business had been surprisingly good today, though the new AC unit still hadn't come in yet, which meant they were making do by propping open the front and back doors—which was fine, until a breeze blew through the magazine stands with a vengeance. She fanned herself with an old invoice, swatting away a mosquito.

"Hey."

She looked up to see Dominic's cousin Jack standing there. *Speaking of annoying insects...*

"Back for more, Jack?" Gianna snapped, folding her arms over her chest. "I'm sure I could scrounge up Dominic or Luca to kick you out."

"Oh, come on, Gianna. I just want to talk. You don't need to call your brother to defend you from the big bad wolf." Jack rolled his eyes, leaning against the counter. "Looks like business is doing well. Though, it'd be nice if you could turn up the AC. It's boiling in here."

She plastered on a smile, trying not to cringe at the mention of the temperature. "Thanks."

"Listen, I just want to save Dominic from wasting his time. He has a good life in Toronto, from what I heard. I'll agree that he has *some* ownership of the bookstore. But I'll buy him out."

"Why do you want the store so bad, Jack?" she said. "What's wrong with your Wall Street life? Why are you back here making trouble?"

"I'm not making trouble. *He's* the one who's always made trouble, ever since he was in college." Jack shook his head. She pursed her lips, irritated by his blithe mention of Emmett's birth as trouble. "You know, it doesn't have to be this hard."

"Dominic is the rightful owner of the bookstore, and there's proof of that."

"You and Dominic are never going to be able to keep this bookstore in business. It's a waste of time. I mean, look at this place. Only a few weeks ago, it was falling apart."

"If you're so good at running a business, Jack, why aren't you already a successful entrepreneur?" she snapped, trying to ignore his dig at the store. "Why do you need to steal your cousin's life and his inheritance?"

He opened his mouth. Then closed it again. While he was trying to form a comeback, Dominic and Emmett appeared behind him. Emmett placed a tray of drinks on the counter before sliding under it and reappearing on the other side. "Look, Gianna, I brought you an iced coffee."

"Thanks, Emmett." She hoped Dominic and Jack's face-off wouldn't be *too* dramatic. "Where's the food?"

Dominic plunked a bag of takeout onto the counter next to the drinks.

Gianna patted the seat next to her for Emmett to sit down. "Let's eat lunch while your dad and Jack talk."

* * *

Dominic handed Jack the letter he'd found in Philip Tang's house.

"Here's the proof that Grandpa left the bookstore to me."

Jack's hand extended to reach for it. Dominic's heart rose to his throat. Would Jack accept it? Would he rip it up, tearing away the last piece of his grandfather that Dominic had, besides the bookstore?

He tried to breathe deeply. Jack, despite all his faults, was a reasonable man. He unfolded it, his eyes scanning the page. As Dominic waited, a flurry of emotions drifted over his cousin's face before it finally settled into one of hardened resignation. "I see."

Dominic didn't feel like gloating or being smug. Instead, he reached out a hand and took the letter back. "I'm sorry."

"No, you're not," Jack said. "Sure, go ahead. I'll agree that you own the place. But how about we do something *above* the books, so to speak?"

Dom stiffened. His cousin had never been one for wordplay. "What do you want now, Jack?"

"I'll make you an offer. You have ownership of the bookstore, and I want to buy it from you." Jack named a sum that would be hard for *anyone* to refuse, let alone Dominic. Up until he'd been laid off, he'd been doing well for himself in Toronto, but rent had been expensive, not to mention the fact that he'd had to work *and* raise his son. The number that Jack named was far above the market value: half a million dollars.

"I'll need some time to think about it." He bit the inside of his cheek, looking away from his cousin. He didn't want the other man to see that there was hope Dominic might actually accept it.

After all, what was there to think about? His cousin's proposal was what he'd wanted when he'd come out here. An easy solution, a way to get what he wanted, what he needed, without any of the complications of running Tang's. Facts and figures ran through his head; Emmett might be seven now, but in no time, he'd go off to college. Wouldn't it be nice to have a nest egg or a rainy-day fund? Though he'd been doing well enough for himself the past seven years, he had always worried about what might happen if there was a crisis or something that insurance wouldn't cover. And his recent unemployment hadn't helped him, forcing him to dig into his emergency savings.

"Don't take too long," Jack said, getting up from the bench. "I'll be leaving town after the fair, so I hope to hear your decision before then."

Dom might be unsure about a lot of things right now, but there was one thing he knew for sure: he had a lot of thinking to do.

Chapter Eighteen

One week after Jack had made his offer to Dominic, Gianna began sketching a rough image in her mind of how she wanted the store's booth to look. Even though she knew plenty of booths would be decorated and well put together, she felt they had a chance at perhaps getting a prize or at least a runner-up in the category of the most beautifully decorated booth. At least, she wanted to believe that.

But in the empty lot behind the store, as she stared at the heavy curtains, folding table and stacks of foldable shelves that would make up the booth design and glanced back down at the page of designs she'd made as references, she realized she was going to need a lot of help in arranging the materials in front of her into an aesthetically pleasing booth.

Walking back into the store, she knocked on the door to their office, where she knew Dominic would be. She wasn't sure when she had started thinking of it as *their* office, only that it didn't just feel like his store or hers. It felt like it belonged to both of them, and she was fiercely protective of it.

"Hey, what's up?" He stood from the desk, where he'd been hunching over the old desktop computer Philip Tang had purchased when the internet was first starting out (the speed, size and noisiness of the device all suggested it was as old as Gianna). He quickly closed whatever tab he'd been looking at, which would've sparked enough curiosity for her to ask him what he'd been looking at if she didn't have bigger things to focus on. Namely, the fair.

"I need your help." She jerked her chin toward the empty lot out back, which was visible through the propped-open door. Dominic had wedged it open to keep the breeze flowing through using a door stopper painted to look like the cover of *War and Peace*, something she'd always found humorous. "We need to start putting together designs for our booth."

He waved a sheet of paper as he followed her into the lot. "I have the booth specifications right here."

There was always a series of rules that needed to be followed, but she'd nearly forgotten about them this year. She skimmed the sheet. The booths' designs had to be family friendly, limited to a certain square footage and had to acknowledge the theme of the fair in some way.

"It's the same every year. Follow my lead, and you'll be fine."

Dominic held out a tape measure that he must have pulled out from the storage closet next to the office that was also a break room. "Shouldn't we go by the rules?"

"Come on, where's your sense of spontaneity?" she said. In all truth, she just hated to do math of any kind. It was her fatal flaw.

"Says the woman who sketched out five different designs for how she wants the booth to look," he said, glancing pointedly at her sketch pad. Dominic's mouth quirked into a teasing grin, but his levity didn't touch his brown eyes.

"That's different." Still, she relented and let him measure the square footage of their booth-slash-table to make sure it fit the proper specifications. "Satisfied?"

"It looks good. How did you want the shelves?" he asked, picking up the wooden shelves with an ease that she'd never be able to replicate. Math and upper-body strength were not her fortes. "Stacked like this, or...?"

"I think they should be in the middle of the table, with a stand in between the stacked shelves so we can display an open book on it." She made a vague hand gesture to demonstrate what she wanted, something she'd picked up from her father. It was, perhaps, the Italian trait she'd most strongly inherited.

Dominic arranged the shelves and stands according to her directions. "What about the curtains?"

"I...hadn't thought about the curtains." How would they hang curtains? On one hand, it would be nice to have some shade on such a hot day, but on the other hand, well, she wasn't looking forward to hauling the heavy curtain rod or attaching it to the table. "If you can think of a way to get them into the design without us having to haul around a curtain rod, be my guest."

Inspiration lit up his somber expression. "I think I have just the thing."

On his way to the storage-slash-break room to get supplies for the booth, Dominic passed by Garrett, who wore a Tang's T-shirt today instead of his usual sci-fi ones. The high schooler nodded at him as he began his shift. The bookstore's employees had become familiar to him now, and the atmosphere of Tang's felt less like a business and more like, well, more like a home.

As he looked for just the thing to attach the curtains to the booth, his phone rang.

He checked the caller ID; it wasn't one of his contacts, but the digits looked familiar. Dominic answered the phone. "Hello?"

"Hi, am I speaking to Dominic Tang?"

"Yes, this is Dominic. Who am I talking to?"

"This is Adrien Bouchard from City Financial in Calgary. You applied for the position of branch manager, correct?" Adrien said.

Dominic sat down, nearly collapsing onto an overturned mop bucket.

"Yes, I did..." Now the memory came back to him. He'd submitted his résumé and a cover letter to the company just a few days after he'd come back to Crabtree. "Are there any updates about the position?"

Surely, they wouldn't call just to thank him for applying and tell him it was filled. Right?

"If you're still interested, we'd like to interview you in person. Do you have any time in the next two weeks to come into our offices? I saw that you're based out of Alberta right now," said Adrien.

"I'd..." He swallowed, his head swimming as he blinked, shielding his eyes from the glare of the early summer sun as it filtered through the skylight. First, there had been Jack's offer to think about. Now, this job opportunity, which had been all he wanted a few weeks ago, was being dropped into his hands. Dominic would be a fool to turn it down, wouldn't he? "I'd love to."

"Great." Adrien named a date that was startlingly familiar to him: the date of Crabtree's annual fair. "Can you be in Calgary at four p.m. on August 1?"

"Yes, of course." His mind already swarmed with thoughts of how he would have to prepare, to find a sitter for Emmett, to...

He'd have to tell Gianna, of course.

"Great talking to you, Dominic. I hope to see you soon," Adrien said.

If he got this job—which it sounded like he very well might—he could be close to his parents while still earning a living. The job would be secure. Stable. Unburdened by broken water pipes and damaged AC units. And with the money from Jack, if he agreed to sell the bookstore, he wouldn't have to worry about money for a while. He could work shorter hours, spend more time with his son and even drive up to Crabtree more often to see his parents. It was the smart thing to do, the reasonable thing to do. There was no reason for him *not* to seize this opportunity or to accept Jack's offer.

Taking a deep breath, Dominic picked up his phone again and texted Jack.

I accept your deal.

Gianna adjusted the placement of the shelves on the table as she wondered what was taking Dominic so long to find the materials for the booth. The store wasn't so big that he could get lost. Though, he had been awfully distant ever since his conversation with Jack last week, but she'd assumed he'd only been discouraged by having such a negative altercation with his cousin.

She finished arranging the shelves and walked back into the store. When she opened the office door, he wasn't there. But she opened the browser tab he'd closed and saw a loan application form.

He was taking out a loan without telling her?

As she skimmed over the information on the page, the office door opened, and Dominic stood in the doorway. The stern look in his eyes made her insides twist themselves into knots.

"Why didn't you tell me you were taking out a small business loan?"

"I'm not," he blurted out. "I was thinking about it, but then I decided not to."

"Is the store really in such poor shape that we need to take out a loan?"

He sighed. "Gianna, I..."

She moved to shut the office door behind them, but he stopped her. Like this wasn't going to be a long conversation.

"The bookstore is going to be in serious financial trouble if we don't get at least a few grand to fix the broken pipe and the air-conditioning. It's a good thing this is a small town and the plumbing guy already agreed to fix it without expecting us to pay immediately. Plus, it's already summer. We're losing a lot of customers without any AC," he said.

"I already know all of that." Heated indignation rose in her chest. "I don't need you to explain it to me—"

"We can't come up with that much money.

Even the store's emergency funds would only cover two-thirds of that."

"You're being pessimistic." She would stick with the bookstore no matter what. Why did he sound like he was jumping off a sinking ship?

"We need to be realistic. Jack has made me an offer—"

"I know, and I hope you told Jack no. I mean, how ridiculous is he?" She rambled on, which meant she was nervous. There had to be a reason why Dominic looked so sad. So serious. So unlike the playful father he was with his son, or the man who'd kissed her and said he'd fight for the bookstore with her. No. The man in front of her was someone else. Someone Gianna didn't know.

"Gianna, I told Jack I would sell him the bookstore."

She blinked once. Twice. Again when the first tear spilled down her cheek. "What?"

"I'm sorry. But I have to do what's right for the store and for my son—"

"What was his offer, Dominic?" She folded her arms over her chest, her throat closing over a sob. Gianna refused to cry in front of him.

This man was every bit as mercenary as she'd thought. He'd only hidden it too well.

"He offered me…" Dominic ran a hand

through his hair, not meeting her eyes. "He offered me half a million dollars."

Her jaw dropped.

"You said you were going to fight for the bookstore!" Her voice cracked, and she hated that she'd believed him. She shoved his chest with one hand, trying to push him away. The office was too small for this conversation. Maybe that was why he was leaving, going on to bigger, better things. Something better than her, better than the bookstore. "You *promised*. You promised to stay until the fair!"

"This was always a possibility, Gianna." His voice had turned cold. Brittle. "We need the money. What he's offering us could save the store."

"Offering *us*?" she repeated. "No, that money isn't going to *us*. It's going to *you*. You're making this decision for *you*, not us."

"Gianna, please. Don't try to change my mind."

"What about…" She shook her head. What was the point of asking about them? Their future? "What about Emmett? He loves it here."

"Children are resilient."

"That doesn't mean you have to hurt them like this."

Pain flashed in his eyes. She regretted saying the words, but it was too late. "I'm not making this decision lightly, Gianna. This isn't a spur-of-the-moment whim or a self-ish choice—"

"Are you sure about that? Because I've seen Emmett at the bookstore and in Crab-tree. He's happy here. Don't you care about that?"

"I care about my son. You're not his mother."

No, she wasn't. But a fraction of her had wanted to be, and now he was driving a stake through that part.

She swallowed. She had gone too far. "I'm sorry, Dominic, but I just don't know why you would abandon the bookstore right now. We've done so much. We're so close to the fair."

"I have to do what's best. Yes, you've turned the bookstore into a community hub, but Jack can make it into a profitable busi-ness. I… I can't."

"You've barely tried." Her voice was thready, on the cusp of disintegrating. "Why can't you stay?"

He shook his head, his eyes expressionless. "I have to go."

Dominic walked out, taking a piece of her with him.

Chapter Nineteen

Dominic sat down at his parents' dinner table with a heavy heart. While he knew he was doing what was best for him and Emmett, he couldn't get the look on Gianna's face out of his mind. Yes, it might be good in the long run, but right now…right now, he was feeling the consequences of getting attached. Again.

Was he trying to leave instead of being left? He chewed on his lower lip, trying not to think too deeply about that.

"Dominic," his mother said, snapping him out of his reverie.

He glanced at the empty seat next to him.

Emmett had eaten already and gone to bed, saying he didn't feel well. His mom had brewed him one of her Chinese herbal soups that promised to fix every ailment known to man while tasting absolutely vile. Emmett had drunk it with a grimace, and Dominic had tucked him into his race-car bed, making sure to hear his son's gentle, deep breathing, which signaled he was asleep, before rejoining his parents at the dinner table.

He'd have to tell Emmett about them leaving and about his decision. Soon. But not tonight.

"Yes, Mom?" He scooped bok choy into his bowl of rice and stared down at the ring-stained wooden table.

"You're being awfully quiet tonight," she said.

His father rested an elbow on the table and cleared his throat. "Livvy, he'll speak about it when he wants to."

His mother seemed to disagree, preferring that Dominic speak when *she* wanted him to. "Why don't you tell me and your father what's wrong?"

Dominic chewed his mouthful of vegetables slowly. "I've decided to sell the bookstore to Jack."

His mom's chopsticks clattered to the table beside her plate. "What do you mean, *sell the bookstore to Jack*?"

"He offered me five hundred grand," he

said, swallowing his food and trying not to feel like he'd sold his soul to his cousin.

"And that's all it took?" his dad asked. His father rarely raised his voice, but when he did, well, it meant something was definitely wrong. "For you to give up on your grandfather's inheritance?"

He cringed. "I'm doing the responsible thing. The bookstore can't go on like this. The cost of the damages, not to mention—"

"I hadn't realized you could see the future," his mother said quietly. Where his father's voice only grew in volume when he was upset, his mother went the opposite direction, becoming more withdrawn, provoking one to pry the words out of her.

"The store is barely in the black," he said. "I don't know how much longer it can last. It's better to cut my losses—"

"Better for who? Just for you? What about Gianna?"

His food felt like a lump of lead in the pit of his stomach. "What about her?"

Their kiss, his promise to help her, all the time they'd spent together—it flashed through his mind, anchoring him to his seat when all he wanted to do was leave. To go back to Toronto. To pretend that these few months had never happened.

Perhaps she didn't deserve to be treated like this. But she deserved better than to work at a bookstore that could barely stay afloat.

"Where will she go? Gianna's worked at Tang's for five years," his mother protested.

"She can work at Marchesi's." He tried to shrug off the words and stab of guilt that came with them. It felt like an elephant was sitting on his shoulders.

"Emmett loves being in Crabtree," his father said. "He's loved every minute of his visit here. You're going to take that from him?"

This hasn't been real life. It's been an escape from it.

He tried to force the words out of his mouth. They wouldn't come.

"We'll visit more," he said. "I have a job interview in Calgary. If I get the job, we'll be closer."

His father shook his head. "If this is your decision, your mother and I will respect it. But we can't sit by and tell you you're doing the right thing."

He sighed. "I know I am."

So why couldn't he justify it to his son?

After dinner, he wired the payment to the

town's plumber for the broken pipe. Then he called the local heating and cooling company again to see when they could come in to make the necessary repairs. It would be paid out of pocket, which was fine, considering the sum he'd receive from Jack in a few days, as soon as his cousin's lawyers finished drawing up the contract. He'd receive far more than the cost of the repairs soon, so it would be no problem to pay for them now.

It would be his parting gift to the bookstore. To Gianna.

He knew she probably wouldn't forgive him or understand. But at least he could give her this.

Gianna trudged down the block toward her parents' house, the dry heat of summer making her wish she'd worn something other than the itchy black T-shirt that made her feel like she was going through her high-school Goth phase for the second time. At first, she didn't know why she'd put it on, even trying to decorate it by throwing on a summer dress over it this morning. But she did know.

She was in mourning. For the bookstore, and for all that she'd thought she would create with Dominic, not only at the bookstore. What they could have created between them.

Try as she might not to sulk, Gianna wanted time to grieve. She certainly didn't want to show up to her family dinner and have them tell her "I told you so" when someone inevitably brought up the bookstore. But missing a family dinner would only result in a barrage of further well-meaning, patronizing questions and concerns.

So she stomped up the steps to her parents' porch, breathing in the scent of the last wild roses blooming on the bushes that the Marchesis had planted along the walkway. Putting a hand on the knob, she shouldn't have been surprised to find that it was unlocked. It always was for family dinners, her parents being too busy in the kitchen to constantly run to the door and let in their three children.

As Gianna shrugged off her denim jacket and slung it over the couch on top of Estella's hoodie, she smelled dinner cooking: black bean sauce, bitter melon with beef, rice and steamed fish with ginger and scallions. She ventured farther into the house and entered the living room to find Estella and Luca fighting over the remote.

"The more things change, the more they

stay the same," she said aloud, smothering a chuckle as she watched Estella argue with Luca about whether to watch sports or reality TV. Despite the pain that weighed on her since Dominic had told her of his decision about the bookstore, her spirits were definitely lifted by her family.

Luca looked up and dropped the remote. Estella celebrated her victory with a silent dance until she accidentally stubbed her toe on the coffee table then fell back onto the sofa.

"Hey, guys." She plopped down on the couch next to Estella and hugged a throw pillow to her chest. "When's dinner?"

As if on cue, Luca's stomach growled. He was looking at her with a strange, almost pitying expression that she didn't appreciate. "Soon."

Estella fidgeted in her seat, playing with the volume on the remote and turning down the TV, which currently displayed one of the contestants sobbing as she poured her heart out for the camera. She didn't particularly enjoy seeing the reminder of her present situation. "How are you, G?"

Before she could help herself, her sadness turned to anger, and the words spilled out of her lips. "Don't pretend to feel sorry for me now that you've heard that Dominic's leaving after the fair because he's selling the bookstore to Jack. Just…don't. I know you never believed in the bookstore, anyway."

Estella's mouth opened, then closed, then opened again. While she performed her best imitation of a goldfish, Luca spoke up, his brown eyes narrowing. He propped himself up with one elbow on the armrest. "I never said that."

"Maybe not, but I know you both thought it." She folded her arms over her chest, unable to back down now. That had always been her greatest weakness. The inability to let go of a fight she couldn't win.

Estella found her voice. "You know everyone in the family likes having you around more, Gianna, but that doesn't mean at the expense of your happiness."

Before she could respond, her mother's voice rang through the house. "Dinner is ready!"

As they filed into the dining room, tension filled the air. It nearly choked Gianna as they sat down to say grace, and she resolved to keep her mouth shut for the rest of dinner.

That pact with herself was immediately

broken, however, when her father looked up at her after they had blessed the meal. "Gianna, I heard about the bookstore. I'm sorry."

"I don't want to talk about it." Her throat closed around the words, and she barely forced down a piece of food, wincing as she bit down on a slice of ginger by mistake.

"Well, you'll need to discuss it eventually," her mother said.

Even if her father *was* sorry to hear about the bookstore going to Jack Tang, he would be happier that she was going to work for the restaurant now. She resigned herself to the same old, same old. After all, wasn't that what Dominic had done? He'd given up on the risky path, taken the easy way out. The safe way out, the one that didn't involve broken AC units and constant fears of hardship.

Maybe she should do the same thing.

Since her food had turned to lead in her stomach after a few more bites, she excused herself. Just as she'd stood to grab the denim jacket she'd thrown over the couch, her father's booming voice reached her ears. "Gianna, I'd like to talk to you after dinner, please."

Sighing, she agreed before walking into the kitchen and rifling through the fridge for dessert. Her parents often brought home left-over pastries, cakes and tarts from Marchesi's, sometimes bringing them to neighbors or the needy, and at other times, eating the food themselves. If she was going to have to talk to her father, she wanted to be armed with sugar first.

Twenty minutes later, she had eaten most of a piece of matcha-flavored Japanese cheesecake and was contemplating her next career options when her father walked in.

He took the seat next to her, and for a moment, they both stared at the backsplash in silence. Then he spoke. "Gianna, you know I love you and your brother and sister very much."

His statement surprised her. While she'd been logically aware of it, it was uncommon for either of her parents to declare their love for their children verbally, preferring to do so through actions.

"I know." She swallowed the last morsel of cheesecake before dabbing at her mouth with a tissue.

"That's the only reason I wanted you to work at Marchesi's." He shook his head. "It's not to control you or ruin your life or—"

"Maybe not," she said, pushing the words

past the lump in her throat that had nothing to do with food. "I know you want what's best for me, Dad. But when you tell me that I *have to* go back to Marchesi's, it feels like you don't believe in me. It feels like you believe that I'll never succeed, or that the bookstore will be a failure, before I even begin. I just wish you could believe in my ability to do something other than a job that's been handed to me by my family."

His brows rose. "Is that what you think of me? That I don't believe in you?"

"Yes." She blurted out the word without meaning it.

It wasn't her father who didn't believe in her. It was Dominic. Dominic, who'd complimented her art, who'd been the only one who did, who'd told her that he'd fight for the bookstore. Dominic, who'd been the only other person who affirmed her belief the bookstore was *worth* fighting for and who'd promised she didn't have to fight for it alone. Dominic, who'd left. Who'd never believed in her or the bookstore at all. She didn't know what hurt more.

"Gianna." Her father's tone was admonishing. "Listen, you still have time before you decide whether to work at the restaurant.

Just because Jack Tang bought the bookstore doesn't mean you have to quit—"

"Jack Tang doesn't care about the bookstore!" Tears welled up in her eyes before she could stop them. "He hasn't even lived here for years. He's been off in New York—"

"And Dominic was in Toronto," her father interjected.

That's different. The words were on the tip of her tongue. Was it different? Dominic was leaving, too. Wasn't he?

"All Jack cares about is turning a profit." Her shoulders sagged as she realized the description might fit Dominic, too. "It feels like I'm the only one who really cares about Tang's."

Her father's voice was comforting but stern. "If you are the only one who cares about Tang's, then don't stand there and watch the bookstore be demolished. The daughter I raised would never just give up, no matter what other people did. If you want the bookstore, Gianna, fight for it. I give you my blessing."

She rested her head on her father's shoulder and held back the rest of her tears. There was no time for crying now. Not when there was work to be done.

* * *

Gianna yawned as she drove toward Tang's the next morning. After burning the candle at both ends, she'd created the perfect design for their booth.

But as she went to park her car in her usual spot, it was taken by an enormous pickup truck. Frowning, she pulled over and got out. Then she spied the words painted on the side of the truck: Harvey's HVAC. This had to be the AC unit being repaired at last.

Her suspicions were confirmed when she marched toward the door and saw a beefy man in a white T-shirt standing outside with his arms crossed.

Summoning her cheeriest smile, she asked, "Hi, can I help you?"

His scowl deepened when he saw her. "I'm John Harvey, from Harvey's HVAC, Heating and Cooling. Is Dominic Tang here?"

"Why do you ask?"

"Well, he booked the delivery of an AC unit plus an all-new ceiling fan to be installed at eight this morning. He hasn't shown up, though. I've been waiting half an hour for someone to let me into the store."

"I'm Gianna, the bookstore's manager. I'll

let you in. Dominic is, ah, busy." *Too busy for the bookstore, it seems.*

"Huh." The man grunted but didn't dissent when she fumbled with the keys to let him inside.

He followed her in as she directed him toward the area where the AC unit and ceiling fan were to be set up. Then, she bustled around the store, trying not to worry about the cost of the improvements. A ceiling fan *would* be nice, especially as it was already summer, but it was another thing to add to their already strained budget.

Finally, unable to spend another moment waiting for customers to arrive and tired of doing inventory, she marched toward the man. "Excuse me, Mr. Harvey? Did you give Dominic a quote of how much this would all cost?" She gestured vaguely toward the AC unit and ceiling fan he was setting up.

"I sure did, and he already wrote me a hefty check for the whole thing."

Her stomach churned as her eyebrows knit together. "He—he did?"

"Yeah, he did." Sighing, clearly frustrated by her questions, the man showed her an invoice. "Paid by Dominic Tang, says right there."

She took the invoice from him, frowning. Dominic had already paid for the repairs to be made, including a new ceiling fan, and he hadn't done so from the store's budget.

He'd done it with his own money.

Yet he'd abandoned the store, anyway. What was going on here?

"Thanks for letting me know." She passed the invoice back to Mr. Harvey, trying to keep her hands from shaking.

The prices of the ceiling fan and AC unit weren't exorbitant, but they were still a hefty sum. So why would he do all this, just to leave the bookstore? Just to leave *her*?

None of it made any sense. But Gianna was determined to get to the bottom of things, if it was the last thing she did...

Chapter Twenty

Dominic stared at the empty guest bedroom he'd been staying in for the past two months. The suitcases he'd brought with him from Toronto were open on the floor. The room had cream walls and a beige bedspread. Devoid of any personality, it was just what he had thought he'd needed when he left Crabtree seven years ago: a fresh start.

All that he needed to do was to meet Jack, sign the agreement and drive to Calgary for his job interview that afternoon.

Now if only he could bring himself to tell his son about it. While he'd informed his parents of his decision—his mother's disappointed resignation had been the hardest to bear, though his father's reaction hadn't been easy to deal with, either—he had yet to tell

Emmett. The heartbreak on his son's face, the anguish in his eyes… That wasn't an image he wanted to conjure up. Nor was it one he wanted to be the cause of.

But he had to. It was the grown-up, responsible thing to do.

Last week, he had told Emmett they were going on a road trip, not telling him where they were going. Emmett had spent all morning guessing, wondering if they were going to drive to Banff or Jasper. However, Dominic still couldn't tell his son the reason they were leaving.

But a part of him was scared that Emmett would talk him out of going. Dominic had already come close to breaking his deal with Jack when he'd spoken to Gianna. Her tearful expression had nearly collapsed something inside of him, knocking down the walls of his resolve. And he couldn't let that happen.

"Emmett!" he called. "Are you ready yet? We're going to leave this afternoon."

By the time they made the two-hour drive to Calgary, Emmett would hopefully be too tired to ask any questions about why they had left. Another frisson of remorse burned in his chest at the thought.

"Emmett?" he said again. He stopped in

front of his son's bedroom door and knocked. "Hey, kiddo, are you awake?"

The door eased open with a creak loud enough to startle any sleeping child. However, when it opened all the way, the room looked empty. The closet doors were ajar. Emmett's little backpack was unzipped and half-filled on the floor next to his unmade race-car bed. The lights were off, and a heap of clothes was strewed over the carpet.

Dominic frowned. Maybe he was in the bathroom? He checked that door, too, and didn't see him.

His parents had already left early this morning to go to the fair, before he'd even woken. The only people in the house were him and Emmett. Or so he'd thought...

"Emmett! This isn't a game. We have to get going. I'm not playing hide-and-seek with you." He turned the house inside out looking for his son. He called his parents, and they confirmed that Emmett wasn't with them, only making his anxiety spike.

His heart throbbed in his chest, his hands balling into fists. What if someone had taken him? What if he'd run out onto the street and gotten hit by a car?

He racked his mind, trying to figure out

where his son might have disappeared to in the small town.

And then it came to Dominic where his son had gone.

Gianna went through the motions of setting up her booth and selling in a daze. Last night, she hadn't been able to sleep, so she'd taken the extra time to bake and decorate cookies to match the books. She was now carefully arranging her stack of books on the booth's table, displaying them beneath the pink-and-white striped awning that barely shielded her from the sun. The extra act of decorating the cookies had taken her mind off of the fact that Dominic was leaving. Today.

She wouldn't even get the chance to say good-bye. She doubted he'd want to hear it from her, anyway. They'd barely spoken since he'd talked to her about his decision. At least Jack hadn't stopped by the bookstore again to gloat. She tried to imagine having Jack as a boss, and failed. It would be a nightmare.

But it was a nightmare she could at least delay until after the fair. Maybe she'd choose an entirely different path and move out to Calgary. The idea of working in a big chain bookstore that sold more candles than books didn't appeal to her, but it would be better than staying in Crabtree after she'd failed.

Failed to convince Dominic to stay. Failed to be enough—failed to make the bookstore enough—so that he'd want to stay. Failed at making the bookstore a thriving business. Her parents had been right, and she'd been wrong. Jack Tang would hollow out any personality from Tang's and gut it just as thoroughly of its character as Dominic had wanted to do when he'd first gotten here.

This was her last-ditch effort. At least if she won the fair's small business prize, she'd have some small consolation, knowing that her efforts had at least garnered some recognition.

She stared down at the cookies in front of her. Some were heart shaped, others book shaped. She snapped on a pair of vinyl gloves and began arranging them in a glass display case she'd borrowed from Marchesi's, trying not to let the grumbling of her stomach dissuade her as she smelled kettle corn and apple pie.

Suddenly, her phone rang. She checked the caller ID before answering and nearly dropped her phone when she saw that it was Dominic. "I'm surprised to hear from you. Calling to say good-bye?"

"Gianna, Emmett is missing. Did he show up at the bookstore?"

"The bookstore's closed." Her spine stiffened. *Emmett is missing?* "For the fair, remember? I'm sorry, but I haven't seen him. Maybe he's here at the fair somewhere. Your parents are here. He could have snuck a ride with them."

"Thank you. I'll drive over right now." Then he hung up abruptly.

Where could Emmett be?

She wanted to join in the search for him, but she had to keep an eye on her booth. Picking up her phone again, she texted a message.

Can you make an announcement? Emmett is missing.

Lillian wrote back right away.

Of course! Hope you find him.

Shortly after, Lillian's voice crackled over the loudspeakers. "Dominic Tang's son, Emmett, has gone missing. If you see a seven-year-old boy with dark hair, please call Dominic's number or let Mrs. Cheng know. Thank you."

The fairgoers began exchanging glances,

which turned into whispers, gossip circulating as quickly as the message had. When a high-school couple stopped by her booth to buy cookies, she heard them wondering aloud if Emmett had run away because he found out that his mother had abandoned him at birth. She was amazed that people could be so cruel.

For the rest of the morning, she sold a few books and some cookies, then decided to take a break for lunch, her growling stomach forcing the rest of her body to go on strike. She texted Dominic.

Any updates on Emmett?

His reply was brief, even curt.

No.

She sighed as she walked over to buy herself a hot dog. Just as she had grabbed the packets of relish and ketchup, Lillian's voice boomed over the loudspeaker again.

"The finalists for the small business prize have been announced. They are as follows: Blooming Bouquets, Carl's Butcher and Tang's Terrific Tomes. If you are running these booths or involved in these businesses, please make your way over to the judging tent so the judges can declare a winner. Thank you."

She was a finalist!

Scarfing down her hot dog, she ran toward the judges' tent and skidded to a halt, wiping her mouth and taking a deep breath before entering. To her surprise, she spied a tall frame by the judges' table and wondered if it was Dominic. Then the figure turned, and she realized it was Jack.

"What are you doing here?" she blurted out before she could stop herself.

"Dominic asked me to come. After all, I will soon be the owner of the bookstore, so any monetary prizes that the bookstore receives will make their way to me."

She narrowed her eyes at him. "Actually, half of the prize money goes to the employee who runs the booth and comes up with the product to enter into the fair."

"Yeah!" Lillian piped up from where she was conversing with her mother, who was coordinating the competition. "It's the rules. Page twenty-seven, section 4B…"

Jack waved a dismissive hand. "Whatever. That means I'll get the other half as soon as Dominic clinches the deal."

She huffed, trying not to let her annoyance

show on her face in front of the other contestants. A tall man she recognized as Carl, the town's butcher—who supplied all of Marchesi's meat—sported a bushy mustache and a jovial expression as he struck up a conversation with Jack. He had been running the butcher shop ever since he'd inherited it from his father, who in turn had inherited it from *his* father. Next to him, Gianna spied Alicia Baker, the owner of a local florist shop, wearing a flower-patterned apron and standing expectantly in front of the table. Walking over to the table, she took her place next to the florist.

Alicia immediately turned to her with a smile. "You're Lil's friend Gianna, right? You always order the pink peonies."

Gianna nodded. "Yes, I love how they brighten up the store."

She tried to brush aside the memory of Dominic bringing her those flowers. It was best not to dwell on a man who would soon be out of her life.

The contestants fell silent as the judges whispered amongst each other, comparing notes on their clipboards. Her pulse ratcheted up, her heart rising into her throat. She rocked back and forth on her heels, waiting for them to announce the results.

"Well, we will soon come to a decision," one of the judges declared. "But first, we'd like to interview the finalists."

It was only then that Gianna noticed the sole journalist, along with a cameraman, in the tent. She vaguely recognized the reporter from prior news broadcasts, as they usually reported small, feel-good stories about saving abandoned puppies or children's fundraising efforts.

The reporter turned to her first. "We're here with the three finalists in the biggest category of Crabtree's annual fair, the prize for the small business who's done the most for the community this year. One business will receive a fifteen-thousand-dollar grand prize. Tell me about your business, miss."

"I'm Gianna Marchesi, the manager of Crabtree's local bookstore, Tang's Terrific Tomes. We've recently experienced a change in ownership since the previous owner passed away, and…" Her throat closed up. She could feel what seemed like a thousand pairs of eyes on her, yet none were the ones she wanted to see. *Dominic's and Emmett's.* "And it's been exciting to see how a small bookstore can really be the heart of a community and foster a love for reading. Tang's isn't just a small business, it's so much more. It's…it's a place where everyone can set aside their differences to come together and learn about one another and those who are different from them, whether that's through a good conversation or a great book."

She took a deep breath, keeping her smile plastered to her cheeks. She could do this. Even if Dominic didn't believe in her or the bookstore, she did. And she knew that this bookstore could and would succeed without him. It had to.

The journalist nodded. "And if you won this prize, what would you do with the money, Gianna?"

"Well, I'd use it to make some repairs to the store. After that, I would invest it in community programs such as our children's reading hour, tutoring sessions for low-income families and more."

"Well, that sounds great, Gianna. Thanks for sharing," the reporter said before turning to interview the other finalists.

She curled her fingers into fists by her sides before quickly unclenching them. Inhaling deeply, she tried not to let her excitement and exhilaration show on her face, keenly aware of Jack's presence next to her.

"That was beautiful," Jack said, his tone imbued with sarcasm. "So heartwarming."

She glared at him. "Do you even care about Crabtree? Why do you even want the bookstore?"

He said nothing, pressing his lips into a flat line. At least Dominic—though he had turned out to be a money-grubbing businessman—had been polite enough not to mock every word she spoke.

"I have as much a right to the bookstore as Dominic does," he said at last in a low voice. "I'm a Tang, too, Gianna."

His words sent a cool shudder down her spine despite the warmth of the day. She fiddled with the bracelet on her wrist as the reporter finished talking to the other finalists. Finally, the judges ushered them out of the judging tent and onto the stage in a neat row to make the final announcement of who had won the small business prize. Barely able to register what was happening, Gianna filed after the other contestants, hardly noticing that Jack slipped away into the crowd.

"Well, after much deliberation, our judges have decided. The winner of this year's small business prize for best contributions to the community is someone who has put in countless hours of hard work, who has given their all not just to their business but to the community at large and who has truly made every Crabtree resident feel at home in their store. The winner is… Tang's Terrific Tomes!" exclaimed the mayor, a petite woman wearing four-inch wedge sandals. "Congratulations, Miss Marchesi."

Blinking rapidly, she made her way toward the front of the stage and accepted the small trophy. "Th-thank you so much."

The crowd clapped and cheered, some hollering for a speech.

"I'm so grateful to the judges for awarding this prize to the bookstore." She smiled so hard her face hurt, but in her heart, beneath all the joy, was an icy sliver of disappointment. *Dominic should be here.* "I'm excited for the future of Tang's, and I'm excited to see how we can work together for the good of the community."

In the crowd, she spotted a curly head of hair, quickly hidden by a Toronto Raptors cap. Gianna frowned.

Is that him?

Before she could stop herself, she spoke into the microphone again. "Emmett!"

A loud series of whispers snaked through

the onlookers, who began nudging one another and gossiping.

"I mean… Um, I'd like to make an important announcement. Emmett Tang, if you're out there, your father is looking for you." Her sunny smile now felt pasted on as she scanned the crowd one more time to see if she had really spotted the young boy or just imagined him while thinking of his father.

There was no sign of Emmett, and her victory tasted bittersweet without him and Dominic here to share it with her.

Frantic and tired, Dominic made his way through the throngs of fairgoers. He wasn't sure he'd ever seen such a large gathering of Crabtree residents before, and he hardly recognized half the faces. Perhaps it was only his panic that made it seem like there were double the amount of people there, but he couldn't help but feel like time and fate were working against him.

After checking in with his parents at his mother's booth, which was next to Gianna's—though she wasn't there, having gone on lunch break—he'd called Emmett's name until his voice was hoarse. His son wasn't at the ball pit or the water-balloon throwing contest or the dive tank. He hadn't gone to the bookstore's booth or the pie-eating contest. Dominic promised himself that when he found his son again, he'd get him a cell phone.

Sighing, he sat back down at Tang's booth. Surveying the cookies and books in front of him, a buzz vibrated his pocket. He pulled out the phone. He had five missed calls from his cousin. He called him back.

"You were supposed to be at my attorney's office three hours ago, Dominic. Listen, I know we're family, but this deal needs to be finalized."

Dominic took a deep breath. "I'm a little distracted right now, Jack. My son is missing."

Static crackled as Dom shifted the phone. "Wow, I'm sorry, man. Have you checked the fair?"

"I've spent all morning doing that."

"When you find him, could you swing by the—"

"I'll cross that bridge when I get to it."

Then he hung up. What was he doing? Had he really made such poor life decisions that his son felt like he had to run away? The notion made him sick to his stomach.

A reminder buzzed on his phone.

Job interview with City Financial in two hours.

He stared down at the ornately decorated books in front of him, and the cookies in their display case. They made the perfect pairing. They complemented each other, each beautifully formed on their own, but together... They made something special. Was that what he'd been running from?

He'd been scared of losing himself, losing his stability, losing his financial security in this bookstore. In this town. In *Gianna*. But what if he was doing the opposite? What if he was losing a piece of himself by running away and going to Calgary? What if he was losing the chance to become part of something greater than himself, the chance to become a family with her?

He leaped to his feet. Dominic knew what he had to do.

The deal is off, he texted Jack, then ran toward the stage.

Gianna finished her speech, walked off the stage and went back to her booth. Just as she reached it, she heard a rustling from beneath the table. Lifting the red cloth she'd draped over it, she saw Emmett. "What are you doing here?"

"I didn't want Dad to find me and take me back to Toronto." His words came out in a panicked rush.

"Sit here," she said, patting the chair next to her. "How long have you been here? You must be thirsty and tired."

He yawned, shaking his head. "I'm not tired. And I'm not coming out until you promise you won't let my dad take me back to Toronto."

She held out an untouched bottle of strawberry lemonade. "Do you want a drink?"

"I want to stay in Crabtree!" He looked close to tears.

Gianna sighed, getting off her chair and crouching in front of Emmett. "If you don't want to go to Toronto, tell him that, kiddo. I know your dad loves you very much, and he just wants to do what's best for you."

He sniffed. "Can I have some lemonade?"

"Only if you get out from underneath the table," she said. "And how did you get here? Everyone's been worried sick about you."

He crawled out and hopped onto the seat next to her. "I snuck a ride in the back of Grandma and Grandpa's car. Then when they got here and started unloading their stuff, I ran into the fair and hid. But when I heard you call my name, I came here and hid in your booth."

She ruffled his hair, sighing. "Promise me you won't run away again."

He gave her a pinkie promise, which she supposed was all she could expect from a seven-year-old boy. Just then, a familiar voice reached her from the loudspeakers.

"Thank you, Gianna, for that great speech," Dominic said, clearing his throat. "But if you'll just give me a few minutes, there's something I'd like to say on behalf of Tang's. After all, I'm still the rightful owner of the store."

She was confused. Hadn't he sold the store to Jack? Her eyes widened as she passed the bottle of lemonade to Emmett.

He saw his father and waved, though Dominic was too far away to see him. "Hey, what's Dad doing up there?"

"I don't know," she said, her brows pinching together.

"If I could have everyone's attention, that would be great," he said. She spied Lillian's bright pink dress as she stepped off the stage and disappeared into the crowd. "Some of you may know me. Probably better than I'd like."

An awkward chuckle rippled through the gathered throngs.

"I'm Dominic Tang. I didn't plan to give this speech. But my son is missing, and I think I know the reason why."

Emmett put down the lemonade and cupped his hands around his face. "I'm not missing! I'm right here!"

The noise of the crowd subsided, but not soon enough for Dominic to hear his son, who got off his chair and began running to his father. She got up to follow him, barely catching up to clutch his hand.

Dominic resumed his speech. "Emmett, if you're out there, I'm sorry. I'm sorry I didn't listen to you when I thought I was doing what was right for our family. Now I know that what's right for us isn't just what I want or what the smart decision seems to be. It's about choosing where we belong, and our hearts—*my* heart—lies with the bookstore."

She nearly tripped over her feet when she heard that.

"Not just with the bookstore, but with one woman who works there," Dominic continued. *Surely, he doesn't mean...*

"Gianna Marchesi, I have to apologize to you, too. I was foolish, and I thought I was doing the right thing, but you were right. I wasn't helping the bookstore. I was abandoning it, and I never want to do that again. I never want to leave *you* again. Gianna, Emmett, I love you, and I never want to be parted from you. Do you think you can ever forgive me?"

When they reached the front of the stage, the people parted for them like the Red Sea parted for Moses. Gianna's smile was so broad it made her cheeks ache.

Emmett hugged his father's side. "Does this mean we're staying in Crabtree?"

"Yeah, kiddo." Dominic mussed his son's hair, but his eyes were fixed on hers. "We're staying, if you'll have us."

"Why did you pay for the bookstore repairs yourself?" she asked him. "You didn't even tell me!"

He didn't let go of her hand. "It was supposed to be a parting gift."

She smacked his shoulder. "I was so confused."

"I was a fool to go behind your back and a fool to leave and a fool to give it all up. I promise in the future, I'll let you know before I make any big financial decisions about the store."

Gianna straightened, rocking back on her heels. "Fine. Then I forgive you."

"And?" Mischief glimmered in his brown eyes.

She wrapped one arm around Emmett and the other around Dominic, reaching up on her tiptoes to whisper, "I love you, too. Both of you."

Those were all the words he needed to hear, apparently, as he leaned down and kissed her.

"Ew! Gross, Dad!" Emmett said.

The gathered crowd laughed, and Gianna smiled, pulling away. "We're right where we belong, aren't we?"

"We sure are." His fingers still interlaced with hers, he gripped Emmett's in his other hand, and together, they walked off the stage.

Epilogue

> If fairy tales exist, I've found my once-upon-a-time start. Love, Dominic

Gianna read the note one final time before tucking it back into the beautiful clothbound classic edition of *Jane Eyre* that had just been delivered to her dressing room. She took a deep breath, staring at the cover, trying not to cry and ruin her makeup.

It was her wedding day, after all.

"Are you ready?" Lillian asked her, for what felt like the millionth time.

"I'm as ready as I'll ever be." Gianna's hands were *not* shaking. Maybe they were a little bit.

"It's okay to be nervous, you know." Next to her, Lillian wore an emerald bridesmaid's dress, her hair pinned up with a gold clip. "It *is* your wedding day. You only get one of those. Plus, Emmett might break something during the ceremony—"

"I think he's outgrown that." He was nine now, and he was far from the boisterous troublemaker he had once been. Though still fairly mischievous, with an impish grin and a prankster's spirit that showed itself in glimpses at the Crabtree elementary school, Emmett was maturing into a young man. "He'll be fine."

"Then what is there to worry about? Dominic's not going to jilt you. You're the best thing that's ever happened to him."

"I could say the same for him," she said with a dreamy sigh. Though it had been two years filled with ups and downs since their first meeting in that bookstore, he'd proposed on her birthday, in the middle of Tang's. A few weeks later, she'd signed the paperwork to adopt Emmett as her own.

"You two are too adorable," Lillian said.

"You're the one who was pushing us to get together!" Gianna craned her neck as she glanced around the dressing room. "Where's Estella?"

"Probably with Emmett. I think he wanted

to play a video game, and she was the only one who agreed to play with him."

She shook her head. "That kid is spoiled."

"He's your kid now," Lillian said with a laugh.

"I know," she said. Soon, it would be official. She and Dominic would be husband and wife. Gianna fanned her face to keep the tears from coming.

"Don't worry, Gianna." Emmett's voice reached her ears, and she turned around. "My dad loves you."

"And what about you?" she asked, her lips curving up in a smile.

"I think you're pretty cool, too."

Estella was right behind him, looking slightly disheveled. "I tried to stop him…"

It was only then that she glanced down to see Emmett's previously neat attire, now soiled with dirt. "What have you been doing, young man?"

The legs of his dress pants and his patent leather shoes were streaked with dirt, and a sheepish grin was on his face. He held something behind his back. "I got you something, Gianna."

"Is it a frog?" One time, she had woken up

to a frog on her pillow when she, Emmett and Dominic had gone camping in the woods.

"No!" he insisted, then pulled out a bouquet of wildflowers. "Dad said you like pink flowers, so I got them for you."

Her heart cracked as she stared at the dirt-covered stems and roots of the brightly colored wildflowers. "They're beautiful. Thank you, Emmett."

Estella huffed, pulling up the skirt of her green dress to reveal her pumps, which were caked in mud. "He could have at least tried to be neater."

"Perfection is overrated." She took the flowers from Emmett and laid them on the table. Then she picked up a makeup wipe, which would have to do. "Now, sit down so I can make you look presentable."

"But Gianna, your dress," Lillian protested. "It's going to get dirty."

She glanced down at the white silk. Then she laid a towel over her skirt and gestured for Emmett to sit across from her on the settee. Gianna patiently dusted the dirt off his laces and slacks until the navy material, at the very least, had no obvious stains, while Estella brushed the mud off her previously pristine shoes.

"Do you like them?" Emmett asked again while she retied his shoes, though she knew perfectly well he was old enough to do it for himself.

"I love them." She glanced over at her bouquet of calla lilies and baby's breath. "Now go find your dad. He'll be wondering where you are."

"Okay." His gap-toothed smile had filled in, and he'd have to get braces soon, but Emmett smiling at her was still the most adorable sight she'd ever seen. "See you at the wedding!"

Gianna gazed in the mirror one last time. A sweetheart neckline with long, lacy sleeves and a train that was neither too long nor too short, her dress flowed smoothly over her figure without being too formfitting. The dress was perfect for her. *Dominic* was perfect for her.

Thank You, God, for all that You've given me. All that You've done for me. May I find some way to spend the rest of my life becoming worthy of Your blessings.

She walked out the door to marry the love of her life.

Dominic took a deep breath as he stood at the altar. He looked forward to seeing his bride. The woman who would shortly become his wife.

Next to him, Emmett was hopping impatiently from one foot to the other.

He frowned and leaned down to whisper, low enough that the pastor wouldn't hear, "Everything all right?"

"Yep," Emmett replied.

His brows furrowed. "Did you lose the rings?"

"They're in my pocket, Dad."

"Did you—"

"Shhh." Luca, standing behind Emmett as the best man, nudged him with an elbow.

Dominic straightened. His gaze was fixed on Gianna, the entire world seeming to fall away at the sight of her. She wore pink flowers in her hair, matching the ones in her bouquet, and when she finally reached him, she shifted the bouquet to one hand to high-five Emmett.

The pastor cleared his throat. "We are gathered here today to celebrate the union of Dominic Tang and Gianna Marchesi…"

With Gianna's hands in his and Emmett standing close by, Dominic felt as if every piece of his life had fallen into place by God's hand.

He had a thriving business in the bookstore that was Tang's. His son was flourishing in Crabtree. And he was about to create a family with the woman he loved.

"Do you, Dominic Philip Tang, take this woman to be your lawfully wedded wife?" the pastor asked him.

"I do." He took the ring from Emmett. Dominic slid the wedding band onto Gianna's finger.

"And do you, Gianna Beatrice Marchesi, take this man to be your lawfully wedded husband?"

"I do." Her smile blinded him. She plucked the ring from Emmett's hands and placed it on his finger.

"I now declare you husband and wife. You may now kiss the bride," the pastor proclaimed.

Dominic leaned down, brushed the veil away from Gianna's face and lifted it over her head. She reached up on her tiptoes and touched her lips to his.

Their kiss was gentle, sweet, the promise of a lifetime's worth of such moments ahead of them. He pulled away, blinking slowly. "I love you, Gianna Tang."

"I love you, too, Dominic Tang," she whispered, her brown eyes wide.

Emmett darted between them and gripped both their hands. "Are we a family now?"

"Yes, we are," Gianna said, grinning ear to ear.

* * * * *

Dear Reader,

While I was born and grew up in Canada, I couldn't resist sprinkling pieces of my Chinese culture and childhood into this book. Growing up, I always longed to read books that featured characters I could relate to, not just emotionally but also culturally. So, I hope that readers can find common ground with Dominic and Gianna, too.

Dominic and Gianna both have trouble finding and/or fulfilling their callings amid other people's expectations for them, and I related to those difficulties, too. I pray that for any reader who is struggling with the same, you would hear God's voice and know He is with you every step of the way.

Feel free to get in touch if you liked the book! You can find me on my website, nicolelamauthor.com.

Best,
Nicole